TANSY'S TITAN
COSMOS' GATEWAY BOOK 3

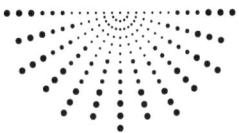

S.E. SMITH

ACKNOWLEDGMENTS

I would like to thank my husband Steve for believing in me and being proud enough of me to give me the courage to follow my dream. I would also like to give a special thank you to my sister and best friend Linda, who not only encouraged me to write but who also read the manuscript.

And a special thanks to Paul Heitsch, David Brenin, Samantha Cook, Suzanne Elise Freeman, and PJ Ochlan—the awesome voices behind my audiobooks!

S.E. Smith

TANSY'S TITAN: COSMOS' GATEWAY BOOK 3
Copyright © 2012 by Susan E. Smith
First E-Book Published November 2012
Cover Design by Melody Simmons
ALL RIGHTS RESERVED: This literary work may not be reproduced or transmitted in any form or by any means, including electronic or photographic reproduction, in whole or in part, without express written permission from the author.

All characters, places, and events in this book are fictitious or have been used fictitiously, and are not to be construed as real. Any resemblance to actual persons living or dead, actual events, locale or organizations are strictly coincidental.

Summary: Tansy has a personal vendetta against some of the worst criminals in the world, and nothing will keep her from bringing them to justice, not even an alien determined to claim her.

ISBN: 9781481273046 (kdp paperback)
ISBN: 978-1-942562-09-2 (eBook)

{1. Romance (love, explicit sexual content). 2. Action/Adventure Thriller. 3. Science Fiction – Aliens, Portal. 4. Paranormal.}

Published by Montana Publishing.
www.montanapublishinghouse.com

CONTENTS

Synopsis	vi
Chapter 1	1
Chapter 2	10
Chapter 3	16
Chapter 4	26
Chapter 5	32
Chapter 6	39
Chapter 7	54
Chapter 8	60
Chapter 9	69
Chapter 10	78
Chapter 11	84
Chapter 12	92
Chapter 13	102
Chapter 14	109
Chapter 15	115
Chapter 16	123
Chapter 17	142
Chapter 18	148
Chapter 19	154
Chapter 20	162
Chapter 21	168
Chapter 22	174
Chapter 23	184
Epilogue	191
Additional Books	195
About the Author	199

SYNOPSIS

A science fiction action/adventure romance that can stand alone!

Tansy Bell, is the middle daughter of the three Bell sisters. She has always been a little different, even for a Bell, but she learned to harness that difference to blend in or stand out just enough to get what she wants—and what she's always wanted is to bring down the worst criminals in the world. She's devoted her life to it, and this time, Tansy is sure she's going to die for it.

Mak 'Tag Krell Manok is the wild one of his four brothers. Few men in any galaxy dare to challenge him, but being tough won't magically make his bond mate appear. He knows he will recognize her immediately, but there are so very few females compatible with Prime males, and Mak returns home from his latest search frustrated—only to discover his oldest brother J'kar has found his bond mate. It seems a portal opened on J'kar's ship, a female 'human' named Tink Bell stepped through, and bonded with J'kar. What is even more astonishing is Mak's reaction to an image of Tink's sister.

So Mak has set a new course: for Earth and the female that stirs his blood to fire! But first, he has to find her. Next, he has to convince her she belongs to him—but if all else fails, he will just take her. After all, she is a delicate little thing, certainly no match for a Prime warrior.

It doesn't take Mak long to discover that a huge amount of trouble can come in a small package, and there is one female in the universe with the strength and determination of twenty Prime warriors who is not afraid to stand up to him—even if she is afraid to love him.

Internationally acclaimed S.E. Smith presents a new story brimming with her signature humor, vivid scenes, and beloved characters. This book is sure to be another fan favorite!

CHAPTER ONE

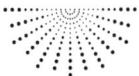

Tansy Bell let her head drop back against the wall she was sitting against and stretched her leg out in front of her. She grimaced as pain and fatigue tried to sink its nasty claws into her. Biting her lip to keep from crying out, she pulled the torn material she was using as a bandage back and looked at the wound on her leg.

Getting shot sucked, Tansy decided, *getting shot twice sucked even more.*

She ignored the wound on her side. It wasn't as bad as the one on her leg. Her shirt was stuck to it anyway and she hoped the bleeding had stopped. She was lucky she wasn't in worse shape than she was considering how many guns had been firing at her.

At least the one on my side is just a flesh wound, she thought tiredly, unlike the wound in her upper thigh.

She choked on the acid filling her throat as she probed the wound, trying to see how far the bullet was embedded. She was pretty sure it wasn't too deep. If it had been, she would never have been able to run at all. A shudder went through her as excruciating pain flared out, radiating through her body in wave after nauseating wave.

"This totally sucks," Tansy whispered as she wiped a stray tear from her cold, clammy face.

She was deep under cover and no one would even acknowledge she existed, much less come to help her. Tansy closed her eyes, waiting for the nausea to pass. She had an emergency medical kit she'd put together, but she didn't relish having to operate on herself, especially in her present environment.

This was not where she wanted to die, but unless she could pull another miracle out of her pocket, it was highly unlikely she would make it out alive. The area was crawling with pissed off bad guys who wanted the information she stole back. They also wanted her as well. Preferably, still alive so they could have fun killing her slowly.

Tansy pulled the backpack she'd dropped earlier closer to her. No sense in putting off the inevitable. If she didn't get the bullet out, she wouldn't heal and it would only hurt worse later.

Not to mention, she thought ruefully, *it is harder than hell trying to run with one moving around in your leg.* She should know because that was exactly what she had been doing for the past couple of hours.

Rummaging around, she pulled the small kit out. It contained a topical and local anesthetic, sterilized kit with a scalpel, sutures, bandages, and antibiotics. Opening it, Tansy focused her mind on what she was doing and not on how much pain she was in. She used her knife to cut the hole in her black pants wider so she could see what she was doing.

Ripping the packaging for the needle open with her teeth, she quickly filled it from the small vial. She numbed the area around the wound before pulling the packaging containing the scalpel and tweezers toward her. Poking the area to see if it was numb enough, she was satisfied she could work on it.

She carefully enlarged the entrance wound, letting the soiled material she had wrapped around it before catch the blood pouring from the wound. Using the tweezers, she felt for the slug. Fortunately, it didn't appear to be that deep or have hit anything major. She carefully pulled it out. Using her forearm, she wiped the sweat from her brow that formed despite the near freezing temperature in the abandoned building she was hiding in.

Blood flowed thick and rich from the wound and Tansy quickly wiped what she could up before picking up the suturing kit and began sewing up the hole in her thigh. Once she was done, she cleaned the area and wrapped a clean, sterile bandage over it before giving herself an antibiotic shot. When she was done, she peeled her shirt from her side and cleaned and bandaged that wound as well. Next, she pulled a regular sewing kit from her bag and sewed the hole in her pants and shirt so it wasn't too noticeable.

Once she was patched up as best she could, she cleaned the area until she was satisfied there was no evidence she had ever been there. She would need to move again once it was dark. She needed to put as much distance as possible between her and the men looking for her.

Tansy grimaced as she put weight on her leg. It was numb now but would hurt like a son-of-a-bitch later. She would need to ration how much pain medication she used. She didn't want anything that might slow her thinking process or to run out in case she might need it later.

If there is a later, she thought, watching through a dirty window as several more cars pulled up and half a dozen men poured out of them. *Time to move, dark or not, if I want to remain alive*, Tansy thought grimly.

Tansy slung the black backpack over her shoulder and tucked a long strand of dark red hair up under the black knit cap covering the rest of her hair. If any of the men saw it, it would be like sending up a flare.

At least Boris liked my hair, Tansy thought cynically.

It was the ace up her sleeve that got her through his door. She didn't think he liked much of anything about her right now, though, including her heavy mane of red hair. She couldn't really blame him. She did steal from him and try to kill his psychopathic ass.

Tansy quietly moved out of the upper level of the condemned apartment building she was using to hide in. *This is filthy, cold, and depressing*, Tansy thought as she moved toward the dark, narrow stairwell, *just like the world I live in*. Tansy gave up believing in fairy tales a long time ago. She didn't believe in any world other than the dark one she was now deeply embedded in. She knew the only way out of it was through death – namely hers. She had made too many enemies over the last five years, both in the States and around the world to ever be left alive.

She wasn't like the rest of her family. She didn't believe in life on other worlds, at least none that she would ever meet, like her dad wrote about, or in the wonder of creating new things like her mom. She didn't have the rosy glasses and love for life that her little sister, Tink, did. If anyone understood her at all it was probably Hannah.

It was Hannah who had unknowingly set the path of Tansy's life. Tansy was determined to cleanse the world of those who took advantage and preyed on the weak. It was Hannah's kidnapping when Tansy was only fourteen that made Tansy realize there was very little good in the world around her. She remembered the haunted look in her older sister's eyes that never seemed to fade after her captivity. Whatever happened to Hannah was enough to drive her to live in the remotest places in the world in order to avoid as much contact as she could with other people.

The men responsible for Hannah's abduction were the first men Tansy went after when she turned eighteen and left home. She knew all the men who were a part of the actual abduction were killed when the local military swept through, but Tansy knew deep down they were just disposable puppets pulled by the strings of someone more powerful.

It took her a year to uncover who it was; a year that changed her life forever. She quickly learned there was an even darker side of life than she could have imagined. She also learned she was not necessarily a good person. She had learned what it meant to kill or be killed. Since then, Tansy had killed many times. She sought the strongest and deadliest teacher she could find and she learned. She also fell in love with him only to lose him to the deadly world she fought against. The man who killed Branson was the first man she killed.

The second man she killed was responsible for the countless deaths of men, women, and children. He used them to sell his drugs, as slave labor for his mines, as prostitutes for himself and his men or to gain even more wealth, and the children… it was the children that finally changed Tansy the most. Her hands shook as she remembered holding the dying little girl in her arms.

Sonya, Tansy thought as she let the rage burn through her, giving her the strength to keep on fighting.

She wrapped the name around her soul so she would never forget why she did what she did. Sonya was only eleven, but Roberto San Juan used her little body for his own sadistic pleasure. She lay beaten and bloody in his bed. He was the man in charge of all the drug cartels in the region where her sister had been taken. Even the military was afraid to touch him.

After the raid at the camp where Hannah was taken, many of the men involved in the raid or their family members were killed because of the attack. Sonya, Tansy later learned, was bought from a Russian white slave trader. Roberto liked young, innocent girls. He used them and discarded them like he did a used tissue. He didn't care who he hurt or killed.

Tansy let her thoughts drift for a moment back to her time in Nicaragua, when she struck out in vengeance against the man who hurt her sister. She had always looked younger than she was, which aided in her infiltration of Roberto's stronghold. At nineteen she could easily pass for being three or four years younger. She had the face of a sweet young girl and the body of a centerfold. It was an explosive combination for a man like Roberto.

Tansy often wondered where she got her different build and coloring from until she saw a picture of her father's mother. She was an exact replica of her grandma Bell. That combination was how she was able to get close to Roberto.

He saw her in the local cantina and wanted her. She was pretending to be on a missionary mission with a small church group who was staying nearby. Within hours of arriving, she was being loaded into his car with two of his guards.

She just pretended to be a scared, confused child. She had to admit she was scared but she was far from confused or a child. She had enough weapons on her to kill the two guards with room to spare. She saved that pleasure for Roberto when he came for her. She let him play with her hair and tell her all the ways he thought she was beautiful and was going to enjoy discovering all her secrets. She let him talk, feeding his ego, and watched him as he poured himself a glass of gin. She did as he commanded at first, removing her dress until she was clad only in her tiny pink panties and matching bra, both very conservative, but alluring in their innocence.

She carefully kept the twin hair sticks holding the poison she would use on him in her thick mane of hair. She wasn't sure how long that would last by the way he was staring at it. She waited until he was close before turning slightly with a tentative smile.

"What are you going to do to me?" Tansy asked in a small, hesitant voice.

Roberto reached out and ran the back of his hand along her smooth, silky cheek. "I might keep you," he said with a thoughtful look. "There is something about you that is… different."

Tansy smiled shyly up at him. He was a breathtakingly handsome man if you could ignore the coldness in his eyes and the cruel twist to his lips. She knew everything there was to know about him. She used the skills her mother taught her on computers to hack into his most private accounts and followed everything he did. At exactly midnight tonight he would be broke. Every penny of his ill-gotten gains would be distributed to charities around the world and to the families of his victims. He would never know it, though. He would already be dead, and Tansy would be far away from here.

"But… what about my family? The missionaries will be looking for me and tell them I am missing," Tansy asked in a slightly husky voice as Roberto ran a kiss along her shoulder.

She shivered as he pushed one of her bra straps to the side. "Your family will be informed you are dead. You belong to me now. I like the taste of you, Julie. You taste wonderful. I wonder what those beautiful lips will feel like wrapped around me," Roberto said moving to cup her breasts from behind in one of his large hands.

Tansy smiled softly before turning in his arms before he could touch her. She licked her lips making sure he was focused on them as she reached her arms up slowly and pulled the sticks from her hair, letting the thick, heavy mane fall down her back almost to her waist. She knew she had Roberto's attention when his eyes flared with desire and his face flushed. Tansy took a step closer to him, letting her arms come down to rest on his shoulders.

"Roberto," Tansy breathed against his lips.

"Yes, my beautiful Julie," Roberto whispered against her lips passionately.

"My lips will never be wrapped around you," Tansy whispered as she quickly jabbed the needle-like end into the side of Roberto's neck and depressed the poison it contained. "And my name is not Julie. My name is Tansy and you have just been erased."

Roberto's eyes widened for a moment, the glass falling from his hand as he started to collapse. He tried to yell out but Tansy covered his mouth with a small tut-tut sound, shaking her head. She helped lower him to the floor where he gazed up at her with a combination of rage and fear.

"This is a much nicer death than you deserve. The poison will make it appear you suffered a heart attack," Tansy said as she moved away from where Roberto lay paralyzed by the poison. "No one can save you. You have terrorized your last victim," Tansy said as she finished dressing in the same clothes the servants wore that she had in the small bag with her.

Pulling out a black wig with gray highlights in it, she quickly and efficiently pinned her hair up tightly against her scalp before sliding it on. She just as quickly added makeup, making it appear she had wrinkles, and the thick, heavy sandals preferred by the older women.

She turned her bag inside out so it looked like a woven basket and deftly filled it with some fruit from a basket on the table. Next, she moved quickly and efficiently around the room wiping anything she had touched with a special cloth designed to remove fingerprints. She used a lint brush to make sure no hair fibers were left either. Moving over to where Roberto was struggling to breathe, she knelt down next to him and tapped his cheek once with a slight smile.

"This is for my sister," Tansy whispered, looking down into his pale, sweaty face. "You should never have messed with my family."

Tansy watched dispassionately as he struggled to say something before his face went slack and his eyes stared blankly up at the ceiling. She was moving out of the sitting room area through to his bedroom when she found Sonya. She knew he had left the girl there so she could watch her die slowly as a warning. She had heard he had done that before, but it was still hard to actually see something like that in real life. There was nothing that could be done for the girl. Tansy could hear the death rattle in her chest from where her lungs were filled with blood. All she could do was sit and hold her, singing one of the childhood songs her mom used to sing to them when they were sick.

Tansy rocked Sonya's lifeless body in her arms for almost ten minutes before she forced herself to gently lay the girl back down on the bloody sheets before covering her. Coldness settled in her heart. It was far worse than even after Branson's death.

At that moment, Tansy knew she would die young because she would not walk away from the Sonyas of the world. She would fight for them until her dying breath. That was how she found herself in the position she was in now. She was after the elusive Russian billionaire Boris Avilov who dealt in the black market. This market included the one who took Sonya from her home and sold her to Roberto four years before.

Tansy came back to the present abruptly when she heard the soft squeak of the stair below her. Moving to the side, she blended into the shadows. She listened carefully to the hushed whispers.

She let a small smile curve her lips as she moved silently down the stairs towards the basement area. There were several doors leading out of the building, but she was interested in the hidden one that would lead her under the streets.

She made sure before she made the hit to know the area like the back of her hand. This little hidden jewel had been buried in the archives of the building department. Branson always taught her to know her prey and to have numerous escape routes.

Always be ahead of them, Tansy. It is the only way you will stay alive, Branson's soft words echoed in her mind.

I know. I miss you, Branson, Tansy thought sadly. *I always will.* Tansy paused as the footsteps moved.

"*Есть ли какой-нибудь признак ее?*" a raspy voice asked in heavily accented Russian if there was any sign of her.

"*Нет, ничто,*" *No, nothing* came the short response. "The doors were still boarded up. We had to break in to get inside. None of the windows were missing boards either," the voice continued to answer him in Russian.

"Check it anyway. Mr. Avilov wants her found and brought to him – alive. He wishes to have the pleasure of killing her personally," the man said harshly.

"Why?" the second man asked. "He usually doesn't dirty his hands with killing... especially the females."

Tansy listened as the man who asked the question received a physical response. "It is not your place to ask why. You will do what you are told," the first man coldly responded.

The only answer was a muffled grunt. Seems like he didn't like the first answer so he wasn't about to ask a second. Tansy moved into one of the rooms off to the side. There was a hole in the floor leading down to the first floor.

She carefully grabbed the long board she had propped inside of it and slid down. She broke out into a sweat as she silently hit the concrete floor harder than she expected. Her leg gave out and she landed heavily on her knee.

Gripping her side and struggling to stand, she limped over to the door. The men were heading up the stairs. She waited until she could hear their footsteps above her before she moved through the bottom rooms.

She stayed in the shadows, not trusting there might not be additional support behind them. Moving on silent feet, she quickly made her way down the hallway and to another set of steps leading to the basement. Ignoring the pain, she slipped into the darkness.

CHAPTER TWO

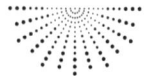

Mak strode into his parents' living quarters looking for his father. He growled out bad-temperedly when he discovered neither of his parents was in residence. In frustration, he walked over to the large bank of windows overlooking the huge palace gardens his mother loved so much. He took deep breaths to try to calm down before he continued his search.

Mak pulled an image out of the front pocket of his vest and looked at it for the hundredth time. He felt the rage burning deep inside him. He wanted the female. He knew she was his. Ever since he saw her image she seemed to take over his every waking and sleeping moment. Not even beating the new warriors in training could tire him enough not to dream about her. He had petitioned the council and his father for permission to bring her here but it was denied. The council was still waiting for Borj to return with his brother's bond mate's mother. In addition, there was concern about the human male who was still at large.

Mak ran his finger over the female's cheek, studying her eyes. There was something in them that called to him. He felt a need to wipe the secrets that haunted her away. The first time he saw her image his whole world seemed to narrow in on her until nothing else mattered but finding her, holding her, protecting her. Never had he felt such strong emotions from just looking at an image.

Tansy, Mak thought, rolling her name over his tongue.

It was an unusual name for an unusual woman. Mak smiled as he let his gaze run over the image he had burned into his memory. She was built with more curves than her sisters. Her hair was a mixture of their red sands and the giant trees surrounding them. Not a bright red, but a dark, rich red with tints of mahogany highlights.

She was looking out at the sea, a far-away look in her eyes like she was deep in thought. The white shirt with long sleeves she was wearing billowed out around her as the wind blew, pulling it back just enough to show hints of the small triangles covering her full breasts. She was wearing short, tan colored pants and thin leather sandals on her feet. But, most of all, it was her expression that haunted Mak. He could see the secrets in her. Secrets he wanted to discover, uncover, and share with her.

"Mak," a soft, feminine voice said. "What is wrong?"

Mak looked up and his expression softened as the female approached him. "Nothing," he said as a small smile curved his lips.

Terra chuckled and shook her head. "I do not believe you. You looked like you wanted to kill someone," Terra said as she peeked at the image Mak was holding. "Who is the female?"

Mak glanced down at the image for a moment before he carefully slid it into the pocket of his vest. "No one," Mak replied gruffly.

Terra just looked at Mak quietly without saying a word. Mak could feel himself groaning inside. He hated it when she did that! It was so much like their mother, Tresa. Whenever either one of the women in his family looked like that at any of them, including their father, the men knew they were doomed.

"It is J'kar's bond mate's sister, Tansy," Mak said reluctantly.

Terra smiled serenely before asking quietly, "You think she could be your bond mate, don't you?"

"I hate it when you do that, you know?" Mak grunted out. "Yes, I know she is my bond mate. It is the only explanation for my reaction to her image."

"How can you know?" Terra asked curiously. "Borj felt the same way about the female he has gone to retrieve. How do you know without the mating rite ceremony?"

Mak shrugged his shoulder before glancing out the window again. "I cannot stop thinking of her. I see her in my dreams and there is an ache deep inside me to see her, touch her that is eating me alive," Mak turned to look at his younger sister tenderly. "I need her and I plan to have her."

Terra shivered as she heard the thread of cold determination in Mak's voice. She wondered vaguely if a male would ever feel that same cold determination to need and want her. She had attended several mating rites ceremonies over the last few years hoping to meet her own bond mate without success. She often wondered if she was destined to remain alone.

It would not be a great sacrifice as long as I have my research, Terra thought.

It was just that since she met Tink, her brother's bond mate, she was more curious. Tink was so different from any female Terra had met before and her physical responses to J'kar often made Terra blush when she was around them. Terra had even noticed a difference in her parents since J'kar brought Tink to their world.

Her mother seemed to have a glow about her and her father... Terra shook her head in frustration. She did not understand what was happening and as a healer and a scientist it was very frustrating to have so many questions and so few answers.

"Then, you must bring her here," Terra finally said.

"Father and the council have denied my request. That is why I am here. I am going to tell father I am going to retrieve the female, with or without his permission," Mak practically snarled out.

Terra laughed, shaking her head. "That is not the right way to approach father."

"What do you suggest then?" Mak bit out in frustration.

"Ask for mother's help," Terra said with a gleam in her eye. "She is learning much from Tink. That is how Borj was able to go. Mother 'persuaded' father," Terra said softly, laying an understanding hand on Mak's arm. "Ask her. She will help you."

Mak hated having to rely on anyone for help. He normally just did what he wanted, but in this case he knew he would need assistance. If he did not have his father and the council's permission, then even if Tansy was his bond mate, they could deny his claim which would be a death sentence to both him and the female he wanted.

He ran his hand over the back of his neck and looked out the window again. His eyes widened as he saw his mother coming out from under one of the huge trees. She faltered a little, her hair was half up and half down and her dress was... ripped? He jerked up closer to the window thinking his mother had been violated by another when he saw his father hurrying out from under the same trees. He was fastening the front of his pants and his shirt looked like it was inside out.

Mak watched in wonder as his father came up behind his mother grabbing her and pressing passionate kisses to her neck. His wonder turned to outright astonishment when he saw one of his mother's hands stroke the front of his father while the other brought his head down to hers.

"I told you," Terra said with a curious smile on her face. "Ever since Tink came here they have been acting different."

Mak realized he was hard as a rock suddenly. Embarrassed for the first time in his life, he didn't want his sister to see that he was extremely turned on by watching his parents' passionate embrace. Instead, he gritted his teeth and nodded to her before leaving quickly.

I need to go beat the shit out of some of the new warriors in a long training session, he thought as he ground his teeth together at the discomfort of his cock rubbing against the front of his pants, *after I stop by my living quarters to relieve some of the pressure first.*

Later that day, Mak learned Borj had returned with not only Tink's sister, Hannah, but her parents as well. Borj was in a lengthy meeting with his father and the council. He thought of his sister's words of advice. Terra was the smartest female he knew, besides his mother. Mak and Terra had always been very close. He was very protective of his sister and would do anything to make sure she was safe and happy.

His mother was the only one who knew about the attempt to steal Terra last year. Even Terra was unaware of it. Tresa had made Mak swear to not tell his father about the incident. She knew if he found out that Teriff would send Terra away to the Isle of the Chosen.

The Isle of the Chosen was a virtual prison for unmated females. The females were sent there to live until mates were found for them, either through the mating rites ceremony, or if none is found before the female reaches the age of thirty cycles, she would be given as a mate during a mating tournament.

Tresa knew Terra would slowly die in such a place. Mak understood his gentle sister and agreed with his mother. The two men who tried to kidnap Terra in the hopes of mating with her died a long and painful death. Their clan's hope of forcing an agreement with the 'Tag Krell Manok clan died with them. Mak felt no remorse at killing the men. They thought nothing of thinking to rape his sister into agreement. Mak had no sympathy or patience for anyone who preyed on those weaker than them. As one of the strongest warriors, he felt it was his duty to protect those who could not protect themselves.

Mak moved down the corridor to his parents' living quarters, rounding the corner just as he saw his mother coming out. He stopped and waited as she approached him. Terra was right. His mother did have a glow about her he had never seen before. There was a spring in her step and her skin and eyes seemed to have an internal light shimmering from her that made him realize just how beautiful she was as a woman. Shaking his head at the strange thoughts he had since seeing the image of the female he wanted, he wondered if he was going soft.

"Why the frown, my son?" Tresa asked softly as she approached him.

Mak shook his head again. "You and Terra are very scary, do you know that?"

Tresa laughed. "Did she give you 'the look'?"

"Yes," Mak grunted out.

"Walk with me. What can I do to help you?" Tresa asked as she wound her arm through Mak's huge forearm. "I am on my way to J'kar's living quarters. I wish to meet Tink's parents and her sister."

"I wish to meet her sister, as well," Mak grumbled out. "But, not the one Borj came back with."

Tresa glanced up at Mak's face. Out of all her children, he was the one she worried the most about and loved dearly. For all his fierceness, there was a gentleness he had for those who were smaller and weaker. He was huge even by Prime standard. Her heart broke as cycle after cycle she would watch during the mating rites ceremony as all the females he was introduced to would shrink back in fear from him. Even the warriors in the palace moved to the other side of the corridor when he walked down one. At almost seven feet of pure muscle, he towered over everyone.

"I believe Tink said her name was Tansy?" Tresa asked gently.

Mak gave a short nod. "Yes. I want her."

Tresa stopped in surprise when she heard the slight desperation in Mak's voice. She looked up into her son's hard, chiseled face for a moment before she smiled. Mak had found his bond mate. There was no doubt in her mind. She just hoped the human female could see beyond his hard exterior and huge form and not be afraid of her son.

"Then, you shall have her," Tresa said with quiet determination. "I will speak with your father."

CHAPTER THREE

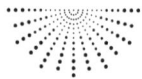

Tansy shivered, tucking her hands under her armpits to try to keep them warm. *Warmth,* she thought as she leaned back against the dirty wall of the abandoned warehouse she was staying in. She didn't think she would ever be warm again.

It had been almost a week since her escape from Boris Avilov's mansion. Tansy was learning real fast the Russian mafia did not like you when you took things from them. They liked you even less when you tried to kill their boss. Her bosses in Washington told her she was on her own. They could not help her. She did, though, need to send them the information she stole as soon as possible. They hoped she understood the importance of the situation and their regret.

Regret my ass, Tansy thought in anger.

She was collateral damage as far as they were concerned. Tansy's job with the government's anti-terrorist division was beginning to piss her off. No wonder they offered such a great retirement plan! No one lived long enough to collect on it.

Boris' goons were thickly spread throughout the region. She stopped trying to count the men following her as they appeared to grow daily. She had hoped he would give up and focus more on damage control between himself and the other bosses. She half suspected some of the men chasing her now were actually from some of those other bosses from the snippets of conversations she overheard.

Whatever was on the microchips must be pretty damn bad, Tansy thought as she listened to the distant sounds of cars moving around the riverside docks of Moscow. *At least it isn't winter,* Tansy thought with cynical humor. If she thought she was cold now, she would really be freezing her ass off.

Her head jerked up when she heard some voices that sounded closer. Pulling herself up the wall, she hissed as her leg throbbed. The wound was beginning to heal, but very slowly thanks to her not being able to rest it. She had torn the stitches out twice since she first put them in.

She was running low on antibiotics, but that was the least of her worries. At the rate she was going, she would either die of exposure, hunger, or a bullet before she died of an infection. Peeking out of the window, she watched as several homeless drunks built a fire in a nearby trash can.

She had made sure when she arrived here late last night that she wasn't seen. Unfortunately, her small stash of rations had been found – by the local rodents. There wasn't much left by the time she retrieved them.

Tansy slid down the wall shaking with fatigue and pain. There was no way out. Every avenue she tried was blocked by Boris' men. There was only one thing left to do. Tansy pulled out the one item she carried everywhere with her.

It was a special satellite phone that she had RITA design and program for her, only her voice could activate the information on it and only if she gave the order using a specific code. Tansy pressed the power on the phone and waited. A moment later she gave the command to activate.

"Uh oh, what's the matter, sweetheart?" RITA asked immediately.

Tansy swallowed the lump in her throat and pushed out the words she dreaded. "RITA, I need you to download some information I am about to send you and upload it to the following computers," Tansy said giving RITA the information in a soft, determined voice.

Tansy inserted the microchip into the base of her minicomputer and attached the cable to her satellite phone. In moments, the information was uploaded. Tansy felt a sense of peace come over her as she realized she had one more thing to do.

"RITA, I need you to set up an immediate conference call with my parents, Tink, and Hannah," Tansy said. "I need you to do it now, no matter what time it is. They should all have their phones with them."

There was a slight pause before RITA replied. "Well, unfortunately, your parents and sisters are out of communication range at this time. I would be more than happy to give your message to them."

"What do you mean 'out of communication range'?" Tansy asked in shock. "We agreed to always have our phones handy. Well, except for me. But, I check it several times a day. Even Hannah…" Tansy's voice faltered for a moment. "RITA, I have to… I need to tell them something important. Please try to contact them. I'll call back in exactly one hour."

"Tansy…" RITA began before Tansy cut her off.

"RITA, I have to tell them goodbye," Tansy said softly. "I have to tell them I love them one last time. Please… one hour."

"I'll do my best, dear," RITA replied.

Tansy pressed the off button and leaned forward. RITA sounded so much like her mom it was more than Tansy could handle in her exhausted state. She laid her head on her knees and let the silent grief consume her. Her slender body shook from the force of her quiet sobs. Pulling her good leg up as close as she could to her body, she closed her eyes, ignoring the freezing wetness on her cheeks and waited to call back one last time. She couldn't leave this world without at least saying goodbye.

Mak stood in the middle of Cosmos' living quarters growling at Derik and Cosmos. Terra was upstairs taking a shower. Mak was doing his normal pacing. They had been there for almost a week. Derik was supposed to return tomorrow morning and he and Cosmos were playing a game of cards. Mak's fists clenched into tight balls as he fought the urge to put one through the wall.

"Why can you not communicate with the one called Tansy? Why do you not tell me about her location?" Mak asked again.

Derik rolled his eyes at Cosmos before laying down a green card. "UNO," he said.

Cosmos looked at the ten cards in his hand and the one in Derik's with a frown. He hated card games. He just did not understand them. When Derik found Tink's UNO cards and wanted to play, he almost decided to plead ignorance as to what they were but RITA had to butt in and tell him. Instead, he had spent the last four days entertaining one teenaged Prime male who wanted to be introduced to every available female under the age of fifty, one huge-ass Prime male who only wanted to know about Tansy, and one frustrating Prime female that drove him nuts!

"Like I told you before, no one can contact Tansy unless it is an absolute emergency," Cosmos said, laying down a card and changing the color to yellow. "She is incommunicado, deep under cover somewhere scary probably. She'll call in a few days when she gets back to the States. She's never gone more than a couple of weeks and always calls at least once a week when she is gone. For all I know, she could have called Tink's phone a hundred times by now."

"She hasn't," RITA said cheerfully. "I always monitor all incoming calls on the phones I designed in case of an emergency."

Cosmos ran his hand through his hair and tried not to look toward the stairwell leading up to Tink's living quarters. He didn't understand it, but the thought of Terra being up there was driving him nuts. He was having a hell of a time concentrating.

"I win!" Derik crowed out as he dropped his last card down on the pile. "You want to play again?"

"No!" Cosmos said grumpily as he threw his cards down. "I think I'll head down to the lab for a little while to do some work."

Mak moved to stand in front of Cosmos as he stood. "I want to know what you mean by incommunicado."

"Listen, Mak. Tansy works for our government doing some kind of shit she doesn't tell anyone about, even her parents. She is a great gal, but no one really knows what she does. She'll call and when she does,

I'll see what I can do. I can't make any promises though," Cosmos said tiredly.

He was beginning to really, really regret building that damn portal! His life was so much simpler before. Cosmos felt his gaze move back toward the stairs leading up again and growled in frustration. He wanted his life back before aliens and unexpected visits and beautiful, aggravating alien females came into it!

"I want her!" Mak growled out in frustration.

"Yeah, you and every Tom, Dick, and Harry with a dick! Have you seen what she looks like in a bikini?" Cosmos asked impatiently. "She's built like a centerfold! Her…"

Cosmos' words were cut short by Mak's hands wrapped around his throat, lifting him off the ground by at least three inches. Cosmos grabbed at the hands holding him and choked. His eyes were glued to the look of pure murder glaring him in the eye. Maybe taking his frustrations out on someone the size of King Kong wasn't a very smart idea. Then again, he seemed to have lost all his ability to think since the female upstairs walked into his life.

"Mak, you cannot kill the human male! Tink would not be happy and neither would her mother who speaks so highly of him," Derik said, putting a hand on Mak's arm to calm him. "Besides, I think Terra would be upset as well."

"Mak!" Terra's soft cry filtered through his brain at last.

Mak's eyes came back into focus as they swung over to where Terra was standing on the edge of the steps looking at him in horror. Mak let his eyes swing back to Cosmos who was beginning to see black spots in front of his eyes. He let his grip relax. Derik grabbed Cosmos around his waist and helped him over to the couch. Mak watched as Terra rushed over to Cosmos. The minute she touched his cheek, she gasped, pulling her hand away and holding it to her chest in confusion.

"Derik, get a cold compress out of the cooling device in the kitchen," Terra said softly looking at Cosmos funny.

"Don't," Cosmos choked out. "I'm okay. I just want to get to my lab."

"Cosmos?" RITA said suddenly.

"Wha…" Cosmos cleared his throat, rubbing it. "What is it, RITA?"

"Tansy called wanting to do a conference call with her parents, Hannah, and Tink. I told her they weren't available," RITA said with a slight pause. "I think she is in trouble. I scanned her voice. It came back showing higher levels of anxiety and something I could not quite analyze… the closest I was able to determine was sadness. She said she wanted to tell her family goodbye… and that she loved them."

Cosmos sat up with a jerk. "Can you contact her?" Cosmos choked out in concern.

"No, her satellite phone is turned off but she said she would call back in approximately forty-two minutes, five seconds and counting," RITA replied.

"Patch her through to the communications system immediately. I don't care when she calls. I want to talk to her!" Cosmos said hoarsely.

Mak looked at Cosmos, frowning. "What is wrong?"

Cosmos looked back at Mak a moment before running his hand through his hair. "I don't know," he said hoarsely still rubbing at his throat. "But, whatever it is, it doesn't sound good. I need a drink. Do you want one?" Cosmos asked with a slight grimace.

"Yes," Mak said looking at Cosmos for a moment before he looked at his sister who was standing to one side frowning down at her hand. "I could use one of the beers you introduced me to if you do not have something stronger."

"I'll take a beer!" Derik said with a grin. "I like it."

Cosmos shook his head. Teenagers, it didn't matter what planet they came from! "Terra, would you like something?" Cosmos asked softly, curling his left hand into a fist.

Terra looked up, startled. Her eyes were bright silver with confusion. She shook her head briefly. Cosmos' eyes followed the flow of her hair as it swung back and forth with the movement. His eyes jerked to Mak's when he heard him clear his throat. Mak was looking at Terra with a small smile on his face.

"I'll go get the beers," Cosmos said gruffly.

"I am tired. I believe I will retire for the night," Terra murmured, looking at Mak briefly before her eyes darted to Cosmos' back as he walked into the kitchenette. "I… don't understand."

Mak walked over to his sister and gently pulled her against him. "You belong with him."

Terra's eyes jerked up to Mak's before she looked down again. "No, it is not possible. He is a human male. He is not strong like a Prime male. He will not be able to protect me like a Prime male can. He..." Terra's eyes moved to her left hand. She opened it slowly to look at the delicate circles showing on her palm. "He is human," she whispered softly.

Mak didn't say anything. He just held Terra for a moment more before she pulled away with a slight, absent-minded nod and walked slowly up the stairs leading to Tink's former living quarters. It was a good thing he didn't kill the human. He would need to talk to him about Tansy, though. If he ever talked about her that way again, he just might.

Mak looked at Derik, who was sitting on the couch playing computerized games and shook his head. He was glad his younger brother was going home tomorrow. He never realized just how much energy it took to keep up with him. Cosmos came in a minute later carrying two beers and a glass with an amber liquid in it. He handed the amber liquid to Mak and sat down next to Derik on the couch, setting the beers on the coffee table and picking up the other game controller. Now this is one thing he did know.

It was time to kick some teenage butt! Cosmos thought as he joined in the battle.

Tansy lifted her head tiredly. She was late in calling back. She had fallen into a light doze after her crying stint. In truth, she had needed both the rest and the cry and not necessarily in that order. She pulled herself stiffly to her feet and checked her perimeter before she moved back to where her backpack was. It was definitely lighter than it had been. She had a couple of power bars, one bottle of water, a few bandages, and some extra rounds of ammo. Pulling the satellite phone out, she turned the power on. She entered the pass code and waited for RITA to pick up.

"Hello dear," RITA said immediately.

"RITA, were you able to get in touch with everyone?" Tansy asked tiredly.

"Tansy, where in the hell are you and what is going on?" Cosmos' voice came on over the phone.

"Cosmos, I need to speak with my family, at least one of them," Tansy said, leaning her head back against the wall.

She pulled her pistol closer to her. She checked to make sure it was fully loaded, just in case. She would save one round for her if it got that bad. She would never let those bastards take her alive. She would still be dead, it would just take a lot, lot longer before she was and she had no intentions of letting them torture her.

"Tansy, they can't talk to you right now," Cosmos said quietly. "Tell me what is going on. You're in trouble, aren't you? Do you need help? Do you want me to come get you?"

Tansy choked back a laugh. Cosmos come get her? The certified genius who has never fired a gun wanted to come and rescue her from the middle of the Russian mafia? If she didn't hurt so much she would have laughed. Instead, a soft sob escaped her before she could hold it back.

"Cosmos, I need you to do me a favor," Tansy said instead of answering him. "I need you to give my family a message for me."

Cosmos felt his gut twist at the anguish in Tansy's voice. Whatever and wherever she was, it wasn't going to be good. He knew what she was up to. He had followed her exploits from the first time he met her, or rather, he had RITA follow them. Her mom and dad knew as well. It was one of the reasons her mom invented RITA. During one of Tansy's brief trips home, Cosmos had to stitch her up from a knife wound. Tilly Bell had given Cosmos a tracking device to insert into her daughter.

"I want to know where she is," Tilly had told Cosmos quietly. "No matter what happens, I want to be able to find her and bring her home."

Cosmos never told Tansy about the small device he implanted into her hip or the fact Tilly and he kept track of her using it. He swallowed down the bile at the thought of having to tell any of Tansy's family something bad had happened to her.

"What is it, Tansy? I'll make sure they get it," Cosmos promised.

"I want you to tell them I'm sorry," Cosmos listened as Tansy took in a deep breath. "Tell them I love them and goodbye for me," Tansy's soft, husky voice pleaded tearfully. "Tell them I always loved them and I'll miss them."

"Tansy, you listen to me. I'm coming for you. Do you hear me? I'm coming for you. You stay alive until I get there," Cosmos snapped out as he paced back and forth clenching and unclenching his fist.

"It's too late for that. I don't have anywhere else to run or hide. It is only a matter of time before I'm found," Tansy said tiredly. "I'm tired, Cosmos. I'm tired and I hurt and I don't want to hurt anymore. I won't go down without a fight but there's not a hell of a lot more fight in me right now."

"Tansy, I know where you are. I can get you out," Cosmos said desperately. "You just have to stay alive until I get there."

Tansy laughed bitterly. "Cosmos, these guys will eat you up and spit you out for breakfast. There are too many of them and they are some of the meanest sons-of-bitches I've ever encountered. It would take a friggin warrior from outer space to whip these guys' asses. I don't think my dad can send me any."

Cosmos smiled and glanced at Mak who looked like he was ready to start tearing things apart with his bare hands. "Well, your dad might not be able to send you any but I can. I'm sending you a really big ass alien named Mak. You stay alive long enough for him to get to you, baby. I promise he can kick all the asses you want plus some."

"Cosmos," Tansy started to say when a loud growl came over the phone. "What the hell was that?" Tansy asked in confusion.

"That is Mak. He is the big ass alien I told you about," Cosmos said, already planning what needed to be done. "I'm serious, Tansy. You stay alive. Just don't kill his ugly ass when he comes to get you, okay? You'll know it's him because he is bigger, badder, and meaner than anyone or anything you've ever seen before."

"How will you find me?" Tansy asked, beginning to feel a sliver of hope blossom inside her.

"I implanted a tracking device in you years ago. Your mom and I always know where you are," Cosmos said huskily.

Tansy took in a deep breath before letting it out. "Thank you, Cosmos."

Cosmos smiled. "Don't thank me, thank your mom. You better keep yourself safe long enough to do it or she is going to be really pissed off at me."

"I'll try," Tansy said before becoming perfectly still. "I have to move. I'm about to have some company."

Tansy quickly ended the call and stood up. She moved stealthily through the dark room toward an old elevator shaft. It looked like she had been found again.

CHAPTER FOUR

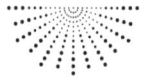

Mak swung around glaring at Cosmos. "What did she mean she was about to have company? What type of company? Why is she calling to say goodbye to her family?" Mak snarled out.

"She is in trouble. Serious trouble that she thinks is going to end badly," Cosmos said already moving toward the stairs leading down to his lab.

He needed to program Tansy's coordinates into the gateway. He didn't know if it would work, but he was going to try to open a portal doorway into the same universe. It would either work or it could… Cosmos' mind was already running with different calculations of what might work and what might go wrong. He was oblivious to Mak and Derik following behind him. He would need to test it out first. The last thing he wanted to do was blow Mak up. That would not be good for public relations between Earth and Baade, not to mention it would piss off Terra and Derik.

Cosmos looked down at his left palm and grimaced at the sight of the intricate circles in the center of it. *Damn,* he thought. Clenching his fist, he tried to ignore the way it burned and itched. Cosmos quickly tapped in the code to enter the lab and moved to the console in the center. Sitting down in the chair, he swung around and began punching in information.

"RITA, I need Tansy's position immediately," Cosmos called out as his fingers flew over the keyboard.

Mak walked up behind Cosmos and grabbed his arm, swinging him around. He leaned down over him and growled out menacingly. "You will tell me what is going on now!" Mak said through clenched teeth.

Cosmos looked up at Mak for a moment before letting his eyes drift over to Derik. Derik gave him a quick nod. Cosmos glanced back up at Mak before replying with a frustrated sigh.

"Sit down and I'll try to explain," Cosmos said quietly, knowing it was better for Mak to know what he was about to be thrown into.

Mak moved away from Cosmos. He leaned back against the railing separating the upper level from the lower one and folded his huge arms across his massive chest. Mak's eyes narrowed as he took in Cosmos' expression. It was very grim compared to the way the human male normally looked.

"From the coordinates RITA has on Tansy it looks like she was in Moscow. That is thousands of miles from here. It would take days, plus lots of red tape, to get to her - days it sounds like she doesn't have. I am going to try to reconfigure the portal to her location so that it opens to where she is. I'm not sure if it will work. I need to run a few tests first. Theoretically, it should but I don't want to take a chance with something going wrong since I have never done it before," Cosmos said quietly.

"Why is she in danger?" Mak asked just as quietly as a slow rage built inside him at the thought of the female he knew to be his bond mate being in trouble.

"Tansy does undercover work for our government. She puts her life on the line every day to try to make our world a better place. She will have to tell you more about it. I just know what I know from the few bits of information I've collected and some of the wounds I've seen on her. Every second longer it takes for me to get this ready means a second less that she might have. She was right about me not being able to do much to help her. I'm a scientist, not a fighter. Whatever is going to be on the other side of the gateway is probably going to be some bad shit. I'm guessing you would know how to handle it," Cosmos added looking at Mak's massive frame.

Mak's smile was enough to cause a shiver to course down Cosmos' spine. "You get me to Tansy and I will take care of anyone trying to harm her," Mak growled out softly.

"I'm going with you!" Derik said, moving up beside his older brother. While he was several cycles younger, he was almost as tall. "I can help you."

"No," Mak growled out, looking sternly at his younger brother.

"No," Cosmos said. "It is going to be difficult enough with one of you guys out there. If the calculations I have figured out in my head work, it will be risky enough. It would be too dangerous trying to keep track of two of you and Tansy."

"You will return home as planned," Mak said sternly. "If you do not return, it may cause problems. They must not know that there is anything wrong here."

"But..." Derik began.

"It is for Terra, Derik. If father or the council feels she is in danger or is not protected here, they will insist she return. If she does, she will be sent to the Isle of the Chosen. Is this what you want for her?" Mak asked his younger brother quietly.

Derik paled at the thought of his beautiful sister being sent to such a place. Even he knew it was little better than a prison. He saw a few of the females that had been sent there at the mating rites ceremony that he snuck into the previous cycle. Their eyes had been empty and they appeared lifeless.

"No, I do not want that for Terra," Derik replied solemnly.

"What the fuck are you talking about?" Cosmos growled out, standing up. "No one is taking Terra anywhere! She stays right here! Where the hell is this Isle of the Chosen?"

Mak looked at Cosmos with a satisfied smile while Derik looked puzzled. "It is an island fortress off the coast. It is a place where the unmated females are sent. It takes the life from them. I've seen the females from there and it is not a good place," Derik said with a frown.

"I would never let them send Terra there. She is too fragile to survive such a place."

Cosmos' eyes narrowed and he could feel a rage unlike anything he ever felt before building inside him. "She stays here. I'll kill any asshole who tries to take her away from me."

"Good. She will stay under your care," Mak said forcefully. "Now, tell me what I need to know to save Tansy."

Over the next four hours, Cosmos and Mak worked out details of what Mak could expect. They went over how to use the modified portable gateway device and what Mak should NOT do when he encountered Tansy. Cosmos had RITA work out several coordinates for them to test the gateway before he felt comfortable enough to do a human test.

"So far most of the fruit we have thrown through the portal has survived. I am going to go through it before I open a gateway to Tansy. I want to do a human trial first," Cosmos said, setting up the gateway again. "I am concerned with the way the energy level keeps dropping off the gateway as soon as the fruit passed through it. Those items are small compared to a human. It may not be able to handle having something of our size."

"But, why does it not have issues going between our worlds, then?" Derik asked.

Cosmos shook his head. "I don't know. I know we don't have a lot of power output like your crystals do. Tink's modifications to the generators helped, but it is impossible for us to keep the amps up for any length of time. There is also some interference of some kind I am trying to work out. I need more time!" Cosmos said in frustration.

"You do not have more time. Tansy could be hurt. Each test you do means more time she is in danger. Open the gateway to her. I will take the chance of finding out if it can handle a larger being," Mak said determinedly.

Cosmos opened his mouth to argue, but the look in Mak's eyes stopped him. He nodded instead. Moving back to the console, he programmed the location showing on the tracking device in Tansy.

"I can't keep the power up for long. You'll have to move as soon as the gateway opens. I'll need at least an hour to get the power levels back up. The fruit has been off by about 10 meters. You'll need to compensate for that as well. Make sure you see an open space before you move through the gateway. I don't want to see you walking inside a wall or over water. From what I can see, Tansy is inside an abandoned warehouse near the riverfront. Keep the satellite phone on you and call as soon as the two of you are safe. I have a couple of friends who live in the area. I'll notify them you need help. I trust them with my life. They will help hide you and get you out safely. Natasha and Helene will do everything they can to help you," Cosmos said as he finished the programming.

He turned and pulled a necklace out of his shirt pocket. Tansy had given it to him last Christmas. It was a miniature spaceship with stars around it made out of platinum and semi-precious jewels.

"Give this to Tansy. She'll know it came from me. Tell her I expect her to return it to me in person," Cosmos said gruffly as he handed the chain and pendant to Mak.

Mak took the offering and placed it in the front pouch of his vest. "I will. I will protect her with my life, Cosmos. You do not need to fear. I will do whatever is necessary to bring her back safely to her family."

"I know," Cosmos grunted out. "If what you feel is half as bad as what I'm feeling toward your sister, I definitely know."

"That is why I am not concerned with leaving her in your care. But be warned, if you hurt her I will enjoy killing you slowly," Mak said with a grin that didn't soften his threat in the least.

"Thanks! I think," Cosmos muttered under his breath. "Are you ready?"

Cosmos looked at Mak and thought that was right up there with the dumbest questions he ever asked. The man in front of him was the largest son-of-a-bitch he had ever seen. On top of that, he was carrying two long swords, two short swords, a CZ 75b semi-automatic 9mm pistol Cosmos had, and a variety of other weapons Cosmos didn't even bother asking about. Cosmos wouldn't let him take his laser pistol stating it was too dangerous should it fall into enemy hands.

Mak grunted his response. He wanted his bond mate. He needed to know she was safe. She had not called back and his gut twisted that he might be too late to save her. Cosmos took a deep breath, gave a sharp nod, and opened the gateway. A burst of light formed before the gateway stabilized and Mak rushed through it. Almost immediately, the gateway disintegrated, leaving empty space where Mak had stood moments ago. Cosmos turned and checked the tracking device he had inserted into Mak, breathing a sigh of relief when he saw it was moving. Mak was at least alive and in one piece.

"He will save her," Derik said from behind him. "He is the strongest warrior I know. He will save her."

"Yeah, but who is going to save him if Tansy doesn't believe him?" Cosmos said, staring at the moving dots on his screen.

CHAPTER FIVE

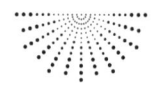

Mak rolled as he felt the punch of energy push him. He lay still for a moment, absorbing what was around him. A sound to the right caused him to shift and move into a crouch, one short sword in his left hand while he pulled several small explosive silver balls into his right. Two old men, dressed in layers of coats with dirty woolen caps on their heads stood around a large burning barrel. Mak could smell the alcohol on them even from ten feet away. One of the men backed up and fell over the curb while the other man just stood frozen as Mak stood to his full height.

"Where is my female?" Mak growled out in a quiet, menacing voice.

The men shook their heads, not understanding. Mak growled low again before remembering the small scanner Cosmos had given him. He pulled it out and looked down to see the signal pointing to the left. Mak snarled a warning to the men and pressed his fingers against his lips before he ran one along his throat, letting them know what would happen if they betrayed him. Both men nodded vigorously at Mak to let him know they would be silent.

Mak turned and looked at the signal again. It was coming from further down the street. He moved along the narrow, dirty street, keeping to the shadows. His eyes searched the darkness for the ones who were after his mate.

He had moved halfway down along one empty warehouse when he caught a slight movement. He paused and watched as a light flared for a few seconds before dimming. He sniffed. He smelled the acidic scent of smoke. Moving silently, he came up behind the figure leaning against a transport. He listened carefully. He needed to make sure there was no one else hiding nearby who could either surprise him or warn others.

Moving up behind the man leaning against the dark transport, he gripped him around his neck, pulling him up over the hood of it and back into the darkness. He held the man up by his throat against the building, ignoring the man's struggles or frantic efforts to breathe. Pulling a device from his belt he held it up to the man's head for a moment.

"You understand me?" Mak asked in a cool voice.

The man nodded in terror. "Да." *Yes.*

Karloff stared into the flaming silver eyes of the man holding him with one hand. He knew what he was looking at was not human. He was huge, over seven feet tall and was too strong to be human. Long canines slowly extended from his mouth as he stared at Karloff as if he were nothing more than an insect.

"Where is my female?" Mak asked.

"What female....?" Karloff choked off as the fingers gripping his throat tightened and the huge man holding him pulled out a sharp, curved knife.

"I will not ask a question twice. Each time you do not answer, I will remove a part of your body," Mak said, letting the blade slice through Karloff's shirt at the shoulder.

He ignored Karloff's jerk as the blade slid through the man's skin almost to the bone. Mac's hand squeezed enough that no sound could escape Karloff's throat. He pulled the blade out and wiped it on the front of Karloff's shirt.

"Do not make a sound except to answer my questions or I will cut out your tongue and let you write the answers out with your blood.

Where is my female?" Mak asked as if he was having a conversation with a friend.

"In the warehouse," Karloff whispered hoarsely.

"How many search for her?" Mak asked coolly.

"There... there are twenty men. Twenty men after her," Karloff whispered back.

"You have served your purpose," Mak said as he squeezed his hand, crushing Karloff's throat.

Mak removed the translator he attached to the side of Karloff's head and pocketed it. He tossed the body into the dark alley. Moving across the open area between the warehouses rapidly, he noticed a set of windows opened on the second level.

He looked around and noticed piping attached to the side of the warehouse. Running, he hit the side of the brick building and jumped up, reaching for the piping about twelve feet off the ground. He grabbed the edge of an open window and pulled himself up.

He slipped his leg over the sill and moved silently inside. He dropped down into a crouch, listening as whispered voices moved outside the open doorway. He straightened along the wall and moved around to stand behind the door. Two men came in. Mak quickly slit both of their throats and disappeared out the door. He worked his way through the level, coming up behind the men and taking them out stealthily. He had dispatched with ten before he heard a shout of warning. The men thought his mate was behind the killings.

∼

Tansy pulled back as far as she could. She had killed five of the sons-of-bitches so far and taken one of the mics so she could listen in but the number of men crawling through the building seemed to be more copious than the rats living in it.

She sucked in a sharp breath as she dropped down onto a lower floor. The last bastard had sliced her across her stomach. It wasn't more than a deep scratch, but it still hurt like hell. Her leg and side was throbbing as well. Over the past week plus, she had lost weight. Her pants had a draw string inside, but the sides were bunching up so much it was making it hard to keep them on.

Tansy leaned down and drew in slow, deep breaths in the hope of pushing away the exhaustion through her mind and body long enough to take as many of these assholes with her as possible. She was out of time, energy, and resources. This was her last holdout. When the men came for her at the last abandoned warehouse she hid at, she escaped down the elevator shaft and made it out using an old coal delivery chute.

They had hounded her every step for the past week and she was working on an hour of sleep here or there, no food to speak of, and rain water. Her body had hit empty and was sucking the bottom of a dry tank. She was down to nine rounds of ammo, eight if she didn't count the one for her. Her only solace was that Cosmos would know where to find her body and bring her home.

Tansy stood up and moved to the door on the middle level of the warehouse. She was done with this shit. She had sent the information to not only her bosses but to RITA and to a friend who worked at the New York Times.

Matt would get it two weeks from the time she sent it. Something smelled about this assignment. It had twisted in her gut and pulled at her since she was first sent out. If her boss or anyone along the path upward was involved with Boris, she would not be the only one going down. She was about to charge out when she heard some of the men shouting in anger and fear.

"Где она? Найдите ее. Сейчас! Отсчитайте!" *Where is she? Find her. Now! Count off!* a deep voice yelled.

"We are missing teams one, three, five, eight, nine, and ten. What the hell is happening? I can't believe that bitch has taken out over half of our men!" a different voice said.

Tansy paused. Over half their men were dead? Who the hell was here? She didn't believe Cosmos when he said he was sending help. Hell, even if he did there was no way someone could have killed another ten men this quickly. Tansy listened as gunfire erupted on the same level as her. A loud roar sent a chill down her spine. *That* had not been human! Screams filled the air before silence took over. Tansy heard frantic whispers over the mic she was wearing. They were down to three men from the sound of it. Maybe she would make it out after all.

~

Mak moved through the level. His shoulder burned where one of the weapons had sliced through, but it was a minor wound that would heal within a couple of hours. He had surprised the two men as they were talking to someone through a device in their ear. He could smell the other three men and was about to go after them when a new scent struck him so hard it almost brought him to his knees.

He smelled blood but it was sweet and tangy. He knew it was his mate's blood and a dark rage filled him at the thought of her being wounded and hunted. He lifted his head and drew in a deep breath. She was on this level, but he could not be exactly sure where. The device he had that tracked her was good to within fifty feet. He was closer than that. He moved out of the room he was in and onto an open platform. He hadn't taken more than a dozen steps when he saw a beam of red light focus on the center of his chest. Cursing at letting his guard down, Mak froze and waited.

"Who are you?" one of the deep voices from before called out.

Mak did not reply. They would not understand him anyway, so he did not bother with wasting his time. He merely looked at the man in front of him while listening to the two coming up quietly from behind.

Karp moved closer, holding his assault rifle up. A wave of cold dread passed through him as he saw the glowing silver eyes of the man standing in front of him. At least, he thought it was a man. He had never seen such a huge bastard in his life. There was a cold calm that belied the fact the man had three weapons aimed at him. It was almost like he knew they could not kill him before he killed them.

"What are you?" Karp asked.

Mak grinned, letting his canines lengthen as he did. He watched the human male standing in front of him pale and fall backwards a step. He could feel his muscles tightening. He would take a couple of bullets probably, but he would kill the men before they could kill him.

Mak watched as Karp opened his mouth. Before he could say a word, a dark figure flew out of the doorway, firing at the man in front of him. At the same time, it hit Mak at waist level with such force, it knocked him sideways into the railing. Gunfire erupted, missing Mak by scant inches. The dark figure rolled and continued firing at the same time.

Mak growled out a warning, wrapped one of his beefy arms around the slender waist and rolled so he was on top. The figure lying under him suddenly went limp. Mak raised up enough to see if the female was alright. She quickly shifted the gun from one hand to the other with a flick of her wrist. She grabbed the back of his head and pulled it down against her chest, firing another two rounds to his right as a bullet whistled by where his head had been.

"Next time, keep your fucking head in the game if you want to keep it attached to your body. Now, if Cosmos sent you, get the fuck off me. If not, I've got a round for you," Tansy growled out, pressing the hot tip of her gun against Mak's temple.

Mak froze as he felt the hot metal against the side of his head press harder the longer he waited. It was difficult for him to move. The body under his was so slight, so fragile he was afraid he would crush her if he put any pressure on her at all.

Mak gingerly rolled off of Tansy. Once he was clear, he rolled to his knees, keeping his hands up, palms forward as Cosmos told him. He let his fingers move slowly to the back of his head in a position to show his mate he meant her no harm.

"I will not hurt you," Mak said softly, staring down into the thin, tired face of his mate.

Tansy bit her lip as she sat up, taking her gun off the figure that even on his knees was almost as tall as she was standing up. She was staring at his eyes. They were glowing. They were silver. They were not fucking human. Neither were his teeth if the fangs hanging down were real.

"Who the fuck are you?" Tansy asked cautiously. "What the fuck are you?"

"I am Mak 'Tag Krell Manok," Mak replied, knowing she couldn't understand him. He looked down at the platform when she asked her last question. Until he was able to insert the translator, she would not understand anything he said. "I am Mak," he repeated instead.

In truth, he was afraid to look into his mate's eyes and see the rejection he had experienced time and time again from the other females as they looked at his massive size and harsh features. He knew this female was his bond mate. She had to be. Even though she had touched him and he did not feel the shock like his brother described, he knew she was his mate. Her voice, her scent, everything about her called to him on a level he had never felt before.

He started when he felt a cool hand under his chin. He slowly lifted his eyes up until he was staring into a pair of dark green ones. It wasn't until she lifted one of her hands that he noticed she was wearing gloves. She bit the end of the glove on her left hand and pulled it off so she could touch his skin.

The moment her hand touched his heated flesh, a shock went through them both. He watched as the pupils in Tansy's green eyes dilated with surprise and her breath caught as she felt it course through her. Her left hand jerked away from him and she clenched it protectively against her chest. Mak slowly let his left hand move from behind his head so he could gently cup the one she was holding against her body in the palm of his. Her whole hand disappeared as he wrapped his larger one around it.

He carefully turned her hand over, letting his gaze drop down to the intricate circles beginning to form in the center. His eyes rose again to meet hers as he slowly brought her hand up to his mouth and pressed his lips to the center of her palm. He would never forget the look in her eyes at that moment. The look in them burned its way down to his soul.

CHAPTER SIX

Tansy swayed dizzily. Her heart seemed to be beating too fast for her to catch her breath. It was like her body was telling her it was okay to shut down for a little while; she no longer had to worry. She tried to shake her head in denial.

No, she thought fiercely, *I can't give in. I can't trust anyone.*

She looked down into dark silver eyes staring up at her in wonder. Cosmos told her the truth. He said he was going to send her a big ass alien warrior to help her and he did. She couldn't understand a damn thing he said, couldn't even think straight enough to understand what the hell happened when she touched him, and could only hope the look in his eyes meant that he really wouldn't hurt her because she was about to crash and burn. Tansy tried to shake her head to clear her vision, but the black spots were growing.

"Help me," she whispered before her body collapsed.

Mak grabbed the slender figure as it melted in front of him. He wrapped his huge arms around her slight figure, pulling it close against the warmth of his body. He stood up, surveying the area. He saw a dark bag just inside the door of the room Tansy had rushed out of. He bent, shifting her in his arms so he could pick it up. Slinging it over his shoulder, he scanned the area carefully.

He needed to get her out of the building. In the distance he could hear the sounds of sirens. Cosmos warned him that neither he nor Tansy could be seen, especially by the local law enforcers. He moved around the dead bodies and headed for a set of metal stairs leading down. He would get her away from the building and assess her injuries. It went against everything in him to wait, but her safety had to come first.

Mak moved silently through the warehouse. He headed toward a large set of doors that opened out back into the dark streets facing the same way he entered. When he reached the metal door, he raised a booted foot, kicking it hard enough to knock it off its hinges and out into the deserted parking lot. He winced when he heard the loud clatter it made when it hit the concrete outside.

He picked up speed once he was outside moving away from the sounds of the approaching sirens. He turned the corner just as the first lights appeared. He continued at a slow, steady run for several blocks until he felt confident he was far enough away from the warehouse they would not be seen. He kept to the shadows and alleys as much as possible. Every once in a while he would bend his head to let his cheek rest along his mate's soft one, wanting to make sure she was still breathing. His arms tightened protectively when he scented the smell of fresh blood on her.

Mak paused to look around him. There was a door leading into an empty office building. Mak moved over to it and twisted the knob. It was locked. With a frustrated growl, he shifted Tansy's slight weight in his arms again and pushed his shoulder against the door. It popped open.

He quickly moved inside and shut the door behind him. It was cold inside, but there was nothing he could do about that. He moved toward a back room so they would not be seen from the street. Pushing through a half-closed door, he saw it was some type of office. An old wooden desk that had seen better days stood in the center of the small room. A broken chair was pushed into a corner. Old papers were scattered along the dirty, concrete floor.

Mak walked over and gently laid Tansy's body down on the desk. He ran his hand over her cheek as a shiver escaped her as she lost the heat from his body. He pulled the dark cap covering her hair off and drew in a swift breath at the beauty of it. The image he had did not do justice to the magnificent color.

Shaking his head to clear it of anything but seeing to her well-being, he quickly moved from her head down to her booted feet. He cursed when he saw the healing wound on her side and the long, shallow cut across her stomach. He quickly cleaned both as best he could with the items he found in the black bag. Once he was done, he pulled her shirt down to cover the chilled flesh.

He continued his examination, pausing when he got to the material in her pants that was stiff with dried blood. He leaned over noticing the material had been stitched together carefully. Pulling his knife out of its sheath, he sliced the material open again, hissing as he saw the red and swollen wound on her leg. The bandage covering it was soaked with fresh blood. The flesh around the narrow strip of material covering it was hot to his touch.

Another shiver racked the slender body and a soft moan escaped the pale lips. Mak's eyes flew to the face of his bond mate. Exhaustion and pain were etched in the pale beauty of it. Dark shadows spread out under the crescent moons of her lashes. Her cheeks were flushed a bright red even as she shivered. Tiny lines formed between her closed eyes and around her mouth at his touch.

He looked down at the wound again. It needed to be cleaned and redressed. He cut through the material wrapped around the wound and cursed silently when he saw the obvious infection. Mak grabbed the bag and dumped the items out on the desk next to Tansy. There was a small satellite phone like the one Cosmos gave him, a small device that looked like a computer, and a small box. Opening the box, Mak found two bandages and a small tube of ointment, nothing else.

Mak reached into the front inside pocket of his vest and pulled out the small kit all warriors carried into battle. Inside were several pain patches, a couple of sealant patches, and a mist with the antigens that killed bacteria and viruses that caused infections. He placed one of the pain patches on the side of his mate's neck and counted to ten slowly.

Reaching down, he sliced through the wound, pulling the few stitches that remained out and letting the infection pour out with the fresh blood. Picking up the HM mist, he sprayed the length of the wound, watching as it foamed up before dissipating. Once it was done, he pulled the skin together and laid a sealant patch over it. It would not come off until the wound was healed.

Satisfied he had done what he could to care for his mate's wounds, he pulled the satellite phone out of his vest and pushed the power button. He quickly spoke the passcode into it and waited for Cosmos to answer.

"Mak, did you find her?" Cosmos' anxious voice sounded immediately.

"Yes," Mak answered.

"Yes, what?" Cosmos practically yelled. "Is she okay? Let me talk to her."

"No," Mak replied. "Is the gateway working?"

"Uh, no. And what did you mean 'no'? Why can't I talk to Tansy?" Cosmos asked anxiously.

Mak looked down at the shivering figure of his mate. He needed to find a warm place where he could bathe her, feed her, and care for her until she was stronger. He needed to take her home!

"She is unconscious. I have cared for her wounds, but she needs additional healing. I must find a place where I can take care of her properly. When will the gateway be working?" Mak asked tersely.

"It is going to be at least forty-eight hours or more before I can get it up and going. The surge of power when you went through it burnt out some of the circuit boards. I have to rebuild them. It also knocked out power to a quarter of the city. I need to work on a different power structure. I've had the power company, the police, and the state calling me bitching about it," Cosmos said in frustration.

"Cosmos, my mate needs care. She is very ill," Mak said quietly. "I worry she will become too weak to survive."

Cosmos released a deep breath that could be heard over the satellite phone clearly. "I've called Natasha and Helene. They are just waiting for the word where to pick you two up. I have your location on the tracking device. Thank God I have backup generators for RITA and some of my other equipment. I'll call them. You'll know it is them. Natasha has dark blonde hair. Helene has short hair. God only knows what color it is this week. Last time I saw her it was blue."

Mak grunted as he put a hand down to still Tansy who was beginning to moan a little louder. "Call them," Mak said and hung up.

He pocketed the satellite phone and gently reached down to draw Tansy's shivering body back against his hard one. He moved over to the wall near the door where he could have a clear view of the door leading out into the street.

His hand shook as he gently raised her left hand up in the dim light until he could see her palm. In the center, the intricate circles of the mating rite were clearly visible. He brought her hand to his mouth and pressed a kiss to the center of it in wonder. She was his! Overwhelming feelings of joy, protectiveness, and possession poured through him until he wanted to roar out a challenge to any who would try to harm her.

He felt her move restlessly in his arms. Pressing a kiss to her hot forehead, he leaned back and watched as her eyes fluttered open. Even in the dim light, he could see they were glassy and unfocused.

"Where... what...," Tansy whispered in a husky voice.

"Shush, you are safe. I will not allow anything to harm you," Mak quietly calmed her.

Tansy frowned up at the huge man holding her. She fought to clear her vision, but she didn't seem to have the strength. She swallowed and turned her head into the warm chest. It felt so good to be held, to feel safe for at least a little while.

"I don't understand you," Tansy muttered softly before letting her eyes close again. "I don't understand...," she said as her voice faded.

Mak cursed. He forgot to implant the translator. He watched as her eyelids fluttered closed again. Her breathing was slower, calmer as well. He needed to give her a massive dose of the HM mist to help with the fever burning through her body.

He felt in his breast pocket until he touched the casing for the translator implant. Pulling it out, he tilted her head to the side. Carefully brushing her thick hair to the side, he inserted the small cylinder into her ear and injected the nano-translator.

He turned her head and repeated the process. He slid the device back into his pocket before reaching for the small medical kit again. Opening it, he removed the HM mist and sprayed it under her nose several times until he felt confident she had received enough. Almost immediately, he felt her body relax as the heat began to fade. Her breathing slipped to a calmer, deeper one, letting him know she had fallen into a deep sleep.

It was almost two hours later that the headlights of a transport lighted up the street. Mak watched as the car slowed and moved down the street a short distance before making a U-turn and parking along the curb across from the building he and Tansy were in.

He rose easily, making sure he didn't disturb Tansy as he stood, watching through narrow eyes. The driver's side door opened and a slender figure emerged. The figure was wearing a thick coat that covered most of the figure's legs. He couldn't see the face that was turned away from him. A fur cap covered the figure's head. A moment later, another figure emerged. This one was wearing a short leather jacket. Short blonde hair with blue spikes were clearly visible.

The figures looked around before the one with the blue spikes nodded before crossing the street toward them. Mak watched as the one wearing the long coat moved down the sidewalk peering into the buildings. He drew back a little as the one with the spiked hair approached with an easy gait. She peered into the window before moving toward the door. Mak palmed one of his short knives. She gripped the handle, pausing when she found it turned easily. She turned and said something softly before moving to enter.

"Hello?" a feminine voice softly called out in accented English. "Tansy... Mak?"

Mak moved out into the door. The female pulled back with a harsh curse in Russian. Mak fought back a smile as she saw his massive size and almost tripped trying to get away from him. He knew she would be able to see his eyes glowing in the dim light. He was still angry and on edge. They would not return to normal until he had his mate in a safe place.

"Your name?" Mak growled out low.

The second female came up and gasped. She muttered a curse as well before her eyes dropped to Tansy. She pushed by the first female, striding forward.

"I am Natasha. Cosmos said you needed help. Come, we do not have much time. Helene will make sure the area is cleared so they do not know you were here. Come, quickly," Natasha said, not coming any closer.

"He is too damn big to fit in my car," Helene muttered. "Where in the hell did Cosmos find him?"

"Hush, Helene. Cleanse the area quickly. Avilov's men and the authorities are not far. It will be difficult enough without you getting pissed off," Natasha muttered as she turned to make sure the road was clear.

"It will be light soon, too," Helene bit out. "He will have to lie down in the back seat. He will draw too much attention otherwise," she whispered back.

Mak watched as the female called Helene cleaned the area with clear expertise. His gaze swiveled back to the one called Natasha. She motioned for him to follow her. He moved quietly, pulling Tansy protectively against him as he let his own eyes scan the deserted streets. Natasha opened the back door and motioned for him to get in.

"You will need to lie down with her on top of you. It is the only way," Natasha said looking around her instead of at him. "We have a fair distance to travel before it gets too light."

Helene hurried forward, opening the front, and threw Tansy's dark bag into the floorboard of the passenger seat. "Hurry, I hear cars coming," she said.

Mak turned and sat down on the back seat. He turned Tansy until she was pressed chest to chest with him. He laid back and scooted until his head was pressed against the far door. Even so, he had to turn his legs at an awkward angle. With a growl, he realized he was far too large to fit into the seat lying down. With a curse, he sat up bending his head so it wouldn't hit the roof.

Natasha shook her head while Helene just frowned. "Why did Cosmos have to send such a large bastard! Sit up but scoot down as far as you can. There is nothing we can do about you now. I will have to get another vehicle," Natasha muttered in anger.

"On it," Helene said, pulling a cellphone out of her pocket and pressing a series of buttons. Within moments, she sat back with a grin. "One will be waiting for us in Kuzetzky."

∽

Natasha grunted as she slid behind the wheel and quickly pulled away, looking in the mirror behind her. She took the first turn she came to before making a series of turns through narrow alleys and along more empty streets. She glanced in the mirror at the huge male sitting in the back of the tiny Lada Priora. Cosmos had warned them that the man and woman they were going to be helping were very special. He forgot to mention the fact at least one of them wasn't fucking human.

This was a first for Natasha and her sister. Both Natasha and her sister owed Cosmos a debt they could never repay. He had saved their parents and two younger brothers several years ago. He used his contacts, money, and expertise with computers to locate them after they had been kidnapped.

Her father was a scientist for the Russian Institute of Research and Development. He was working on a highly secretive program for the government. When Natasha and Helene's mother and little brothers were kidnapped and held in an effort to get her father to give copies of the research over to the American company wanting the technology, they did not know what to do.

Her father, distraught at the loss of his family, had contacted Cosmos for help. Cosmos had met their father at a research conference. Cosmos was able to rescue their mother and brothers, and exposed the company and the men behind it. The American government quickly moved in, shutting the company down. Cosmos used his resources to help their little brothers attend college in England while offering her parents a chance to work for one of the research companies he owned in Prague. Natasha and Helene had been attending college at the time in Paris and he assigned security guards to them. Since then, both of them had returned to Moscow and worked with the Ministry of Internal Affairs.

"Who are you and where are you from?" Natasha asked as she took another turn.

Mak reached into his pocket and pulled out the translator. Helene turned and looked at him suspiciously. He motioned for her to put it against her ear and press the end before handing it to her.

Helene reached for the device. She carefully turned it over in her hand before glancing at the huge man who was hunched protectively over the woman in his lap. He returned her stare with steady silver flames burning in them. She slowly reached up and placed it against her left ear. Mak nodded.

"I am called Mak 'Tag Krell Manok. You may call me Mak," he said in a deep voice. "I thank you for your assistance to myself and my mate. I need to get her somewhere safe so I can examine her more thoroughly."

Helene jerked the device away from her ear. She turned and muttered in a low voice to Natasha who glanced in the mirror in surprise. "Ask him where he comes from."

"Baade," Mak said, understanding what Natasha was saying. "I am Prime," he replied. "Have her place the device against her ear. It will embed a translator so she may understand what I say," Mak watched as Helene place the device against Natasha's right ear and pressed the end. Natasha jerked and looked at her sister in surprise.

"Where is that?" Helene asked, turning to stare closer at the huge man.

Mak shrugged. "Far away. In a distant star system from your own."

"How did you get here?" Natasha asked nervously as she realized she now understood what he was saying. "Why are you here? What do you want?"

Mak looked at the dark brown eyes staring at him periodically in the mirror. "I cannot tell you how I came to your world. It would be too dangerous. I came for my woman. My bond mate. I want… need her," Mak said, gently pushing a strand of dark red hair back from Tansy's temple. He ran his fingers gently over her cheek until he could cup her jaw and pull it toward his chest.

"You came for a woman?" Helene repeated Mak's answer in disbelief.

Mak looked up fiercely causing Helene to lean back in alarm. "She is not just a woman. She is my bond mate. I would give my life to protect her. I will kill anyone who threatens her."

Natasha's eyes widened at the deep, dangerous growl in Mak's voice. She didn't need a translator to know what he was saying. The way he touched the tiny female in his arms and held her so tenderly was enough evidence to tell her he meant it when he promised to kill anyone who would mess with her.

A soft moan escaped the female in question. Natasha watched as the woman's eyelashes fluttered before she opened her eyes. The woman's body stiffened in alarm briefly before she forced herself to relax. She turned her head and her eyes collided with Natasha's in the mirror. Natasha felt a shiver go down her spine.

Shit, Natasha thought, *the woman is almost as bad as the man.*

∽

Tansy forced her body to relax. She could tell the arms holding her tightened the moment she moved. Her quick glance took in all the information she needed to know. She was in a Lada Priora, a popular car in this area of Moscow. There were two females, in addition to the huge ass alien male who was holding her. Tansy recognized the two females. They were Pavel Baskov's two daughters. She remembered their faces from when she helped Cosmos a couple of years ago.

"Which…" Tansy began before clearing her throat and starting over again. "Which one of you is Natasha and which is Helene?" she asked in Russian.

Helene jerked around and glared at Tansy. "How do you know about us?" she demanded.

Mak's head jerked up and a low rumble escaped at the tone in Helene's voice. She jerked back again as far as her seat belt would let her. His eyes warned her to be careful how she talked to Tansy.

Tansy looked up at the face above her. She shook her head. Only Cosmos could find a planet with a Neanderthal on it to rescue her. She turned her head back to the woman with the short spiky blue hair.

"I saw your pictures when I helped get your mom and brothers out," Tansy said, relaxing back against the warm chest and lap. She figured she could move in a little while. Right now, she was just too comfortable. "Cosmos called me in when they were kidnapped."

Helene sat forward, a smile lighting up her face. "You are the female who they talked about! I am Helene and this is my sister, Natasha. All of the reports we were able to get our hands on said only that a female agent of the American government was responsible for rescuing our mother and brothers. They said you were critically wounded," Helene said hesitantly.

Tansy shook her head. "It was a cover-up. They didn't want my cover blown for another assignment I was on. It pulled the suspicion off of me," Tansy said with a sigh as she tried to sit up.

She frowned up at the huge man holding her when he shifted so she was still lying against him. She decided it wasn't worth the effort to fight and relaxed back against his firm chest. She leaned her head back against his shoulder with a tired sigh.

"Where are we going?" Tansy asked.

"We are heading to pick up another vehicle. Your friend is too large to remain hidden and will draw too much attention. Once we have it, we are going to a small farm outside of the city. You should be safe there for a few days. Cosmos is working on a plan to return you to his home. We will be working on a secondary method of escape should his plan fail," Natasha said, pulling up to a line of vehicles.

She nodded to Helene who climbed out of the car. They all watched as she walked across the street to where a man was waiting for her. They talked briefly before she turned and strode over to where a small transport van was parked. Within moments, she pulled out and drove slowly by them, heading down the street.

"Where does she go?" Mak asked harshly, a dark tone of mistrust in his voice.

Tansy's head jerked around so fast her head hit his chin. "Ouch!" she yelped, raising a hand to rub her head. "I can understand you!" she breathed out, startled.

Mak pulled her hand down and looked in displeasure at her head. He brushed a kiss across it tenderly before he pulled back and scowled down at her. "You must be more careful. I have not had a chance to heal your other wounds and you get more. You must not get hurt," Mak growled out fiercely.

Tansy looked up in disbelief. "*Who* are you?!" she muttered.

Natasha chuckled. "I would guess he has decided you are his."

Tansy's head swiveled until she was looking at the back of Natasha's head with a scowl of her own. "Why would you say something like that?"

Natasha glanced briefly at Tansy in the rearview mirror, her eyes danced with merriment. "Oh, I don't know. It could have been his 'I came for my woman' comment or the fact he called you his 'bond mate'."

Tansy's scowl deepened until it was just as dark and fierce as Mak's had been. "I am not anybody's woman and I am definitely not someone's mate. I think I would know if I was," Tansy muttered darkly.

Natasha pulled into a parking space behind a business before replying. "I have a feeling the huge male holding you would disagree rather fiercely with you," she said with a laugh as she opened the door to the car. "Come, we do not have much time before the early morning workers begin to arrive."

Tansy moved to scoot out of the strong arms holding her. For an instant they tightened around her in warning. Tansy shot a glare over her shoulder only to freeze in confusion. The eyes staring back at her held worry and concern.

"Wait for me to get out first. I want to make sure it is safe," the deep voice rumbled lowly.

Tansy shook her head even as she moved over onto the seat so he could get out first. Never in her life had she let someone else take the chance in a dangerous situation. She watched as he untangled his huge body from the back seat of the little car and looked around carefully before bending and offering her his hand. Tansy felt a flutter in her stomach as she placed her smaller hand in his larger one.

Strong fingers closed around her hand and pulled her toward his hard body. Tansy looked down in surprise when she felt the cool air against her thigh. She barely had time to glance down and notice her pant leg was cut open again before she was on her feet in the frigid air.

"Hurry, I will get your bag. Climb in the back of the van," Natasha said, quickly looking around. "Helene says you are very popular with all the wrong people, Tansy. I would be most interested to know what you did to upset not only Boris Avilov but half of the other mob bosses of Russia as well."

Tansy snorted. "Take your pick. They don't like it when you steal from them and they definitely don't like it when you try to kill one of them."

Natasha looked at Tansy like she had lost her mind. "Shit, you don't do anything halfway, do you?"

"Let's go! Sasha said half the force is being called in. There is a warehouse full of dead bodies and the captain is being told it must be contained," Helene said in a hushed tone.

Mak didn't wait for Tansy to begin moving; he simply swung her up into his arms and moved toward the back of the van where Helene was standing impatiently. Natasha moved forward, tossing Tansy's backpack in behind them. She slid into the passenger seat this time while Helene took over the driving.

"Sasha will come for the car in a few minutes. He wanted to make sure we were not followed," Helene said.

"What did you tell your friend?" Tansy asked in a low voice.

She had learned a long time ago the more people involved the more likely there was a weak link in the chain. Someone could always get to one of those links and break it. Whether it was through money, threats, or force it didn't matter. The more people involved the more chance of getting caught.

Helene looked behind her before turning to face forward. "Nothing. Sasha was told we are moving some furniture and needed to borrow a van. I told him I was being followed and didn't want anyone to know where I was moving. I asked him to come get the car and drop it off at the department and I would pick it up later."

"Why would he think you were being followed?" Tansy asked in a suspicious voice.

Natasha turned and looked at Tansy with a mischievous grin. "You are not the only one who brings out a possessive feeling. Helene has an admirer who has been very persistent lately."

Helene snorted. "I should just kill his ass. No one would ever know."

Natasha laughed. "He is only one of the wealthiest men in Moscow. He owns several popular night clubs in the city, as well as in several other European countries. He took a liking to Helene during one of our assignments. Since then, he has been very insistent."

Helene's eyes flashed with irritation. "He is a dirty old man who wants a trophy on his arm. I am no man's trophy!" she snapped out, taking a turn a little faster than she should have.

Mak wrapped his arm around Tansy's smaller body and gripped a metal bar to keep them from being thrown around in the back of the van. "Slow down or drive better. You will not endanger my mate!"

Tansy pushed on Mak's arm in irritation. "I am not your mate. I don't even know who you are! You came into my life a grand total of a few hours ago," she growled back.

"You are mine!" Mak said stubbornly. "You bear my mating mark."

"What in the hell are you talking about?" Tansy glared furiously. "So help me, if you did anything screwy to me while I was out, I'll castrate your ass!"

It took a moment before the words translated correctly for Mak to understand what Tansy said. When it did, he couldn't suppress the chuckle that escaped. "My ass does not have anything for you to castrate. You would need to focus on the front of me."

Tansy's jaw dropped open before snapping shut when Natasha and Helene burst out laughing. "Well, it is nice to know you are built like a man," she muttered.

Mak's eyes gleamed with desire as he leaned close to Tansy so only she could hear his next words. "Oh, I am most definitely built like a man... a very large man who wants you very badly."

Tansy blushed to the roots of her red hair. She looked up at Mak with a combination of shock, fury, and curiosity. Her eyes sparkled at the challenge in his. She refused to back down. She knew what he was doing. He was daring her to be afraid of him. He was daring her to be intimidated by his size. Well, she may have never met a bigger man in size, but she had yet to meet anything that she was so afraid of she would back down.

"Well, just to let you know, I am NOT going to make it easy for you," she whispered fiercely. "I'm not afraid of you, big guy. You can huff and puff all you want, but this little girl is not going to be blown away by you!"

Mak's eyes softened as he saw the stubborn tilt of her chin. "I am counting on that, *je talli*."

Tansy's pulse jerked at the unfamiliar words. "What does that mean?"

"You are my heart. Without you, I would not have a heart," Mak replied, reaching out to gently touch Tansy's chest.

Tansy shook her head, a deep frown darkening her face. "Do you really expect me to believe you? You just met me. How can I be your anything?"

"I have known you for many, many weeks. It has taken that long for me to get permission to come to your world. I have also spent over a week with your friend Cosmos. He gave me this to give to you. He said he wanted it back," Mak corrected in a low tone as he pulled the pendant she had given Cosmos out and handed it to her. "The first time I saw your image I knew you belonged to me, forever," he added quietly.

Tansy stared in silence at the huge alien male who suddenly seemed to be a permanent part of her life. Her heart beat out an erratic pattern until he touched her chest. She actually felt the moment when her heart slowed down to match his. In that instant, she knew that more than their hearts were beating as one.

CHAPTER SEVEN

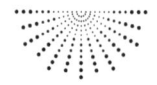

"We have to return to the city. All available personnel have been requested to be present. I would bet all the money Boris Avilov has that it is about the warehouse," Natasha said as she showed Tansy around the small farmhouse. "This belongs to my family. We visit here, but do not live here full time any longer. Helene and I have made some improvements. There are weapons in the pantry here and an additional exit from the basement. Helene is showing Mak it now. I apologize that we cannot stay longer, but we do not want to draw any suspicion to ourselves," Natasha said as she pulled a false wall loose in the back of the pantry to show where numerous handguns and assault rifles hung.

Tansy whistled under her breath at the impressive display of weapons. "You talk about me! These are some pretty exciting weapons you have," Tansy muttered.

Natasha smiled. "After what happened to our mother and brothers, Helene and I are rather careful about being prepared for any contingency."

Tansy nodded as she pulled a couple of Baikal IJ-70 Makarov pistols out. She quickly checked the chamber and clip before reaching for several additional clips. She would need to return to the pantry after she ate and rested. She liked the look of several of the knives.

"I am glad you like what you see," Natasha teased.

"Natasha, we need to get going," Helene called out as she came into the kitchen. "Sasha called. The boss is asking about us."

Natasha nodded before she turned and briefly studied Tansy. With a shrug, she pulled Tansy into her arms for a quick hug. "We owe you more than we can ever repay. Cosmos gave us your satellite phone number. We will contact you when we have additional information. Until then, rest. There are clothes in the bedroom that should fit you well enough."

Helene came over and gave Tansy a brief hug as well. "There is a Land Rover in the shed out back. The tunnel in the basement leads to it. Your man knows how to access everything. Stay inside as much as possible."

Tansy pulled back and looked at the two sisters who were regarding her with worried expressions on their faces. "Thank you for your help. You know that by helping me you have put not only yourselves in danger but your family as well."

Helene waved her hand in the air nonchalantly. "Cosmos added additional security for our parents and brothers. Natasha and I are used to danger," Helene said. "There is plenty of canned food for you. Get some rest."

Mak came into the kitchen where he towered above the three women. His eyes were glued to Tansy's slight form. He had spent time outside checking over the perimeter of the property and listening to what Helene told him about the safeguards set up at the farm. Now, he only wanted the other two women to leave so he could concentrate on healing and caring for his mate. He didn't like the dark shadows under her eyes or the lines of pain that still pulled at her mouth despite the pain patch he put on her. She needed rest.

Mak moved to one side as the two women turned to leave. "You will not tell anyone of Tansy being here," he ordered.

Helene rolled her eyes while Natasha bit back a chuckle. "No, we will not tell anyone. We will call if we find out anything. In the meantime, take care of your woman. She needs rest."

Both women chuckled at Tansy's snort of aggravation. Tansy watched as the two women walked out to the transport van and climbed in. She did not turn around until they had turned onto the main road. With a sigh, she pushed back her fatigue. She needed to check the house and surrounding area out for herself. She wouldn't be able to relax until she knew what was in place and had covered every single possible entry and exit point.

Turning, she ran into a huge muscular chest and a set of equally large arms. She looked up, trying to not show her exasperation at the big man crowding her space. She was going to have to teach him there is a line as to how close he was to get to her. He was currently way over it on the wrong side.

"Okay Mak, is it?" Tansy said, taking a step back, only to find herself trapped by the door. "Listen, we need to discuss this personal space invasion."

Mak tilted his head and looked down into the vibrant green eyes of his mate. "You need food, a bath, and bed," he said. "I will fix you something to eat."

Tansy sighed heavily. "Yes, I agree I need all three but first I need to make sure we are safe. I am going to check out the perimeter of the property and the house before I do any of that. Once I feel we are safe, I'll find something to eat, grab a quick shower, and maybe catch a couple of hours of sleep."

"No," Mak said, crossing his arms and spreading his legs so Tansy was trapped.

Tansy's frown turned into a dark scowl. "I beg your pardon?" she bit out through gritted teeth.

"No," Mak repeated, ignoring the warning in Tansy's eyes. "I have already checked the perimeter. It is secure. You will eat, bathe, and sleep."

"Mak, listen to me carefully," Tansy said, pointing a finger into his massive chest. "I don't take orders from anyone. I haven't in a long, long time. I will eat when I want, bathe when I want, and sleep when I want. You don't want to make me mad at you. Understand? You won't like me very much if you make me mad," Tansy said, making sure she emphasized each point carefully so there could be no misunderstandings.

Mak unfolded his arms and caught Tansy's small hand in his. "You are undernourished. You have dark circles under your eyes from lack of sleep and I can see how exhausted you are. You also have dirt on your face and I need to check your injuries. I did what I could, but I was not able to care for you properly," Mak said, gently rubbing his thumb over the back of her hand.

Tansy bit back a curse as she jerked her hand away from his. Why the hell did it feel so good, so right whenever the big guy touched her? It was more than pissing her off. Emotions were dangerous. Caring for someone only got you killed, or worse, they got the person you cared about killed. She had to get it through his head that Cosmos may have sent him to help her, but that didn't mean she belonged to him.

"Look, I know Cosmos found you, but just because you came along and helped me out does not mean I belong to you. You seem like a really nice guy. I'm sure there are hordes of girls out there that would be happy to be your whatever, but I'm just not the settling down type. Guys who hang with me have a tendency to end up dead," Tansy said honestly. "That's why they don't even give me a partner anymore. No one wanted to take a chance."

Tansy didn't wait for an answer from him. She turned and gripped the doorknob, yanked it open and disappeared outside. She needed some space. Her body was running on empty both physically and mentally.

She thought she was going to die back there in the warehouse. She had psyched herself up for it. When she heard the commotion over the headset about the men dropping like flies, she hadn't believed it at first. There was no way Cosmos could have sent help for her in just a couple of hours. Then she had caught a glimpse of the huge dark figure on the platform. When she heard the one man ask what the hell the massive figure was, she knew he must be Cosmos' supposed alien warrior come to rescue her.

Her heart jerked uncomfortably in her chest and she rubbed at it when she remembered seeing the sights line up on his chest and back. She didn't stop to think of the consequences. She used every one of the bullets left in her gun on the bastards, including the one she was saving for herself.

Never! a deep voice echoed in her head. *You will never take your own life. You will do whatever you have to do to stay alive. I will never leave you.*

What the…. Tansy thought, dropping to the ground near the outside shed and pulling one of the pistols she took earlier. She looked around frantically. Her eyes darted from one spot to the other. Had those sons of bitches done something to her when she was out? She could have sworn they were dead. She rose slowly onto one knee before standing the rest of the way when she didn't see anyone.

I must be losing my mind, Tansy thought, running a shaky hand through her long length of hair. *I've finally gone insane.*

No, not insane, je talli. But, you do need food and rest. Come to me. Let me care for you, Mak's deeply accented voice came through clearly this time.

Tansy bit her lip in uncertainty. *How can you talk to me like this? What did you do to me when I was passed out?*

You do not need to fear me, Mak's sad voice floated through her mind. *I never want you to fear me.*

Tansy didn't reply. She turned around, making sure she kept her mind blank and marched back toward the house. She didn't even say a word when she saw him standing outside, watching her from the corner. She caught herself right before she slammed the door in his face. Mak pushed it open and followed her inside. Tansy remained silent until she was in the center of the kitchen. Only then did she turn around and look at him.

"I don't know how you can talk to me in my head," Tansy raised her hand when he started to speak. "Right now, I really don't give a damn how or why you can. I am too tired to deal with it. But, let us get one thing perfectly clear," she said, taking a step closer as she stared into his wary dark silver eyes. "I… am… not… afraid… of… you. Not now, not when I first saw you, not ever. Do you understand? You might be big, you might be an alien, but I will *never* be afraid of you."

Mak's heart lurched with each word Tansy carefully enunciated. He couldn't have taken his eyes off her if his life depended on it at that moment. He had never seen anything so beautiful as this tiny human female daring him to think she could even be remotely intimidated or frightened of him. Mak watched the fire in her eyes as she looked up at him. It was as if she was challenging him to prove her wrong.

For the first time in his long life, Mak wasn't sure what to do. His first thought was to gather her close, but he feared showing her too much physical affection. Females, with the exception of his brother J'kar's mate and now his mother, did not care for being touched.

He had been with his share of females when he was off-world at the pleasure houses and knew females merely tolerated it. Those females did not care about his size as long as he paid the asking price. There had even been a few women on Prime who had agreed to be with him for a price or a favor. But they had always looked at him with fear and loathing.

He did not see fear in Tansy's eyes. He took a stumbling step back as she walked determinedly toward him. He bumped into the door behind, startled. No, he saw something else, and it did not bode well for him if he disagreed with her.

"Don't you ever, and I mean ever, think I am afraid of you," Tansy snapped out right before she reached up and pulled his head down far enough to give him a hard kiss on the lips.

CHAPTER EIGHT

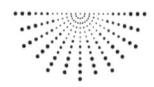

*T*ansy leaned forward, letting the hot water run down over her shoulders. She rested her forehead against the wall and groaned in enjoyment and frustration; enjoyment at the hot water and the feeling of being clean again, frustration at her feelings for a certain huge-ass alien male who was making her insides quiver with emotions she didn't totally understand. A shiver ran through her body as she tried to decide just how big of an idiot she was for kissing him.

Why did I have to kiss the big guy? Tansy thought tiredly. *It just makes things more difficult.*

Why do you think that, je talli? Mak's deep voice echoed in her mind.

Tansy's head jerked up and she scowled at the wall of the shower in irritation. *Get out of my head! I'm having a private conversation with myself right now and I don't need you in the middle of it.*

Why not? Mak asked.

Why not? Why not? Because... Tansy's tired brain refused to go behind that. *Just because!*

Tansy was so tired it took everything in her just to remain upright. She was shaky from fatigue and lack of food. She reached up to try to push her hair back, but even it was too heavy for her suddenly weak arms. She let her head fall forward again and let the tears come. It helped a little. She didn't ever remember being so tired in her life. If only she could just slip to the floor of the shower and let the hot spray run over her for a few hours. If only...

"You could ask for help. I would not think you weak if you were to do so," Mak's quiet voice shook her out of her mini-pity party.

Tansy's head jerked up and she swayed dangerously at the sudden movement. "What are you doing in here?"

Mak smiled as he pulled the shower curtain back and climbed into the shower with her. "And where in the hell are your clothes?" Tansy choked out as her eyes grew wider at the sight of all those rippling muscles covered by a dark, olive skin.

"I cannot very well wear my clothes in the bathing stall. I would have nothing to put on afterwards. You need help. I will care for you," Mak said, reaching for one of the containers on the small shelf inside the shower. He opened it and sniffed. Pleased with his discovery, he poured a little into the palm of his hand and turned toward Tansy. "Turn with your back to me. I will wash your hair for you. If you need to brace your arms on the wall, then do so. I will care for you now."

Tansy stared at the huge male in the shower with her in confusion and disbelief. She was too tired to deal with this. Turning back around to face the wall again, she braced her shaking arms against it before leaning forward slightly.

She moaned softly when she felt his strong fingers working the shampoo into her thick hair. Between the hot water and his fingers, she melted back against him. Soon, it was only his arm around her waist holding her up. He picked up the bar of soap and ran it gently over her skin. Tansy quit thinking. She didn't care that they were both naked. She didn't care that she really didn't know him. She wouldn't have cared if the world ended at that moment as long as he continued to clean her with a tenderness she hadn't felt in years.

She was half asleep when Mak reached around her and turned the shower off. He lifted her carefully and stepped out of the shower, uncaring of the water dripping on the floor. He grabbed a couple of the towels off the counter and walked out of the bathroom. He paused, looking down the hallway. He moved toward the door that was open and found it contained a full size bed. It would be small for him, but he was more concerned with Tansy. He gently laid her down on the bedspread before he began to dry her. He watched as goose bumps formed on her arms and legs from the chilly air. Reaching down, he grabbed a quilted comforter at the foot of the bed and draped it over her.

"I have to dry my hair," Tansy slurred out without opening her eyes. "If I don't…"

"Shush, I will dry it," Mak replied quietly.

"'Kay," Tansy murmured with a deep sigh.

Mak carefully dried the thick reddish-brown locks, marveling at the different colors appearing as he did so. After he was satisfied it was as dry as he could get it with the towel, he picked up a brush off a nearby table and began brushing it out. Tansy didn't move, even when he gently lifted her up in his arms so he could brush the back of it. Once he was done, he pulled the covers of the bedspread back so he could lay her on the crisp, cool sheets.

Mak frowned as he took in the bruises marring Tansy's pale, thin shoulders. He moved her hair to one side and bit back a curse when he saw the faded scar on her left shoulder blade. Deciding he needed to see if she had any other injuries before he brought up the soup he warmed up for her, he pulled the quilted comforter back a little at a time trying to keep her as covered as possible so she wouldn't get cold.

Her body was a patchwork of different colored bruises. She had the wound on her right side just above her hip that was still red and angry. There was a long shallow cut about ten centimeters long that ran across her lower abdomen at a forty-five degree angle showing she had moved just in time as the blade was coming at her.

Mak ran his fingers lightly over her ribs, which were showing. Rage filled him at the thought of how long it had been since she had eaten. The fact that she was so exhausted that she couldn't even stay awake long enough to eat burned through him.

Never again, he swore to himself. *Never again would she put herself through such stress. Never again would she come so close to dying. And,* he vowed, *never again would she feel she needed to save a method to kill herself so she could not be taken.*

He continued his examination of her body, pausing when he

reached the wound he had covered earlier with the sealant patch. The skin around it looked much better. It was no longer red, swollen, and hot to the touch. By morning, it should be completely healed.

Mak rose off the bed and returned to the bathroom where he left his clothes. He pulled his pants on and reached into his vest for his MED kit before he returned to Tansy. He replaced the pain patch with a new one and sprayed a light mist of HM over the cut on her stomach and her side. He did not want to use any more of the sealant patches in case she needed it later.

He covered her with the quilt, tucking it firmly around her before going down to the kitchen. He would reheat the soup and wake her long enough to eat. Then, he would let her rest. Her body and mind needed it. He could feel the fatigue pulling at her when he touched her mind earlier.

Mak gazed down at the intricate circles on the palm of his hand. A shudder went through him as he remembered his first touch with her. The shock to his system was unlike anything he had ever experienced before. He felt his cock harden at the memory and groaned.

He would need to wait to claim her. She needed rest and care, not a horny Prime male right now. He would heal her, claim her, and return with her to his world where he could keep her safe.

He moved over to the stove and turned the burner on under the pot of soup he had warmed up earlier. It had taken him a few minutes to figure out where everything was but he often cooked at home so it wasn't that difficult. He warmed the soup up enough so it could be eaten without burning Tansy's mouth. Pouring it into a bowl, he pulled a spoon out of the kitchen drawer. He carefully balanced the bowl of soup and a glass of water as he moved back up the stairs. He wanted to make sure she had something to eat before he let her sleep. Once she was done, he would check the perimeter of the farmhouse again before he joined her.

He stepped through the door and moved quietly over to the bed. The only thing she had moved was her arm, which was thrown out to the side. Mak couldn't get over how beautiful she looked lying with her hair spread out over the crisp white of the pillowcase.

His body jerked in reaction, but he quickly gave himself a mental rebuke. The dark shadows and clear exhaustion were too evident to ignore. He set the soup and water down on the small nightstand and gently pulled Tansy into his arms.

"*Je talli*, you must wake enough to eat something. Then, you may sleep all you wish," Mak said soothingly. "Come, little one, open your eyes for just a little longer."

"Don't want to," Tansy mumbled sleepily. "Five more minutes, just five more minutes."

Mak chuckled. "Eat the soup I have fixed you and drink some water and I will give you all the five minutes you wish," he promised tenderly.

Tansy's head fell back into the curve of his arm. She forced her eyes open until they were narrow slits and peered through her lashes up at the man holding her. She snuggled closer to him as the chill in the room moved around where the covers had fallen from her shoulders. She was about to tell him she wasn't hungry, but the combination of the determined look on his face and her nose picking up the delicious smell helped her decide to give in.

"I don't know if I have the strength to even pick up the spoon right now," Tansy said honestly.

"You do not have to," Mak said as he helped her into a sitting position against the headboard of the bed. He tucked the covers firmly over her breasts with a muttered curse. "I will feed you."

Tansy sat back against the pillows, a small, sad smile curving her lips. "Why are you helping me? You know it will only get you hurt or killed, don't you?" she whispered, fighting to keep her eyes open.

"Open," Mak growled out in a low voice as he held the spoon to her lips.

Tansy groaned as the warm soup slid down her throat and hit her empty stomach. The warmth seemed to spread out and suddenly she was famished. She leaned forward eagerly for the next spoonful, opening her mouth like a little bird.

"Damn, but that tastes so good," she moaned out.

"When is the last time you had nourishment?" Mak asked gruffly as he spooned bite after bite into her open mouth.

"I don't remember," Tansy answered, looking at Mak with a

muddled expression. "I ran out of power bars three, maybe four days ago. I can't really remember," she said suddenly full and fading fast again. "I can't eat any more right now. I need to get some sleep. If you can wake me in a couple of hours I would appreciate it."

"Drink some water first," Mak said, holding the glass to her lips so she didn't have a choice.

He didn't give her a chance to refuse as he tipped the glass up enough for some of the cool liquid to slide down her throat. She was dehydrated. He would do what he had to do to take care of her, even if it meant bullying her a little. Only when he was satisfied she had drunk enough did he pull the glass away from her lips.

"What did you do to my leg?" Tansy asked after she had drunk half the glass. "It doesn't hurt anymore."

"You were fevered. Your leg was infected. I reopened the wound, cleansed it, sprayed it with a healing mist, and used a pain and sealant patch on you. I also gave you a heavier dose of HM mist to help your body heal faster," Mak said, setting the glass back next to the nearly empty bowl of soup.

Tansy slid back down under the covers, yawning. "I need to get a truck load of the stuff. It would be great to have the next time I get stabbed or shot."

Mak's eyes flashed with fire, but he bit back the retort he was about to make. They would talk about the fact there was NOT going to be a next time if he had any way of preventing it. He wanted to get her out of this world that was so dangerous.

It tore him up to think about a knife or other weapon cutting through her delicate skin. He saw the faded scars from other wounds. It was amazing she had survived this long.

"Sleep," he replied quietly. "I will make sure you are safe."

His words fell on deaf ears. Tansy was already asleep before her head was all the way down on the pillow. She let out a deep sigh in her sleep and rolled onto her side, curling into a little ball. Mak ran his hand down over her silky hair before he leaned over and gently kissed her cheek.

"Sleep tight, *je talli*," Mak whispered. "I will protect you with my life."

∼

Mak finished checking the perimeter of the small farm. It was not very big, less than ten acres. The house was surrounded by thick woods with a long narrow driveway leading to the highway. The wood covering was both good and bad. It allowed the house to remain relatively unseen and provided ample cover, but it also made it difficult to see if any intruders approached.

Natasha and Helene must have thought of that as they set up sensors around the property high enough most animals would not trip it but low enough a human walking would. Helene had shown the sensors to Mak and given him a small tablet PC programmed to indicate when and where a sensor was activated. He carried it with him now, moving and watching as the lights lit up.

He made two passes around the property before he was satisfied everything was clear. Moving back into the farmhouse, he checked each of the windows. The bottom floor of the house consisted of four rooms, a kitchen, a large living area, a small bathroom, and another small room that was set up as an office.

Once satisfied, he moved quietly up the narrow stairs to the upper level. It contained three bedrooms and one bathroom. The bathroom was off the main hallway with one large bedroom across from it and two smaller bedrooms on the same side. Tansy was in the larger bedroom. Mak glanced through the open door.

He caught a peek of her dark red hair before moving further down the hallway to check the two smaller rooms. He opened one door and looked in. There was a small single bed, a nightstand, an armoire, and a chair in the corner. He walked over to the small, narrow window and checked to make sure it was secure.

He moved out to check the last room. It was set up the same way. He checked the window, pausing as a movement outside caught his attention. His eyes narrowed in on it and he waited. Within a few minutes, the dark shape of a deer appeared. It took cautious steps forward, looking around before lowering its head to feed on some of the grass around the house.

Mak released the breath he didn't even realize he was holding. He had been fearful he would need to wake Tansy and move her. She desperately needed rest and care.

I need to get her somewhere safe, somewhere I can protect her, Mak thought in frustration, *I need to take her to my home.*

He reached for the satellite phone Cosmos had given him. Quickly powering it on, he waited impatiently for Cosmos to answer.

"Hello dear," RITA's cheerful voice said.

Mak grunted. "Where's Cosmos?" he growled out.

"Mak, I'm here," Cosmos said breathlessly. "I… uh…. Are you and Tansy safe?"

"I need to get her out of here. She is still in danger. When will you have the portal open?" Mak demanded in a quiet voice.

"Well, there is a slight problem," Cosmos said.

"What do you mean there is a slight problem?" Mak bit out harshly.

"I've run additional calculations on using the portal to transport you from one spot on Earth to another. It isn't safe. All my calculations are coming back with disturbing conclusions. The interference I told you about the first time is a type of natural barrier. It is like trying to go from positive to positive or negative to negative. A natural barrier prevents the two from connecting. If I try to force it, it becomes unstable to the point it is dangerous. That is why it took more and more power each time to push the items through and why the power grid failed as soon as you passed through. It becomes stronger with each passage. I worry it can cause a disruption that could alter the natural flow, becoming explosive," Cosmos explained.

"Why does it not happen between our worlds?" Mak asked impatiently.

"When the portal opens from our world to yours it is more like going from positive to negative where they attract each other," Cosmos said.

"What does this mean?" Mak ground out.

"It means I have to get you home the old-fashioned way. I have Natasha and Helene working on getting a jet. Helene is a pilot and will be able to charter it. It may take a couple of days as they are getting you and Tansy some papers together. You both need to hang low until everything is in place," Cosmos said.

Mak ran his hand through his hair in frustration. He should have brought his portal device with him, but Cosmos had been afraid it would fall into the wrong hands. Now, he was without any means of getting his mate to safety. He had never relied on someone else to help him before and it went against everything in him to do so now.

"Get whatever you need together as soon as possible. I want my mate out of here," Mak told Cosmos in a voice that promised retribution if anything happened to Tansy.

"I will. Give me forty-eight hours and I'll have you both out of there," Cosmos promised before hanging up.

Mak stared out the window to where the deer were grazing. His mind was not on it though; it was on the danger to his mate. He would kill anyone who tried to harm her.

CHAPTER NINE

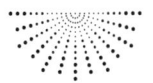

Tansy woke, making sure to keep her body completely still as she assessed her surroundings and her body. She felt almost normal. She was hungry, but she ignored that. She did a brief analysis of her body. Her leg didn't hurt at all, neither did her side or stomach which surprised her. She drew in a shallow breath catching the scents around her. She could smell the clean sheets and…

Turning her head, her eyes widened as she took in the relaxed face of the huge male next to her. He hadn't been a figment of her imagination. She clenched her fists to keep her hands from reaching out. She had the most overwhelming desire to run her fingers along the sharp edges of his face.

She studied his features with a critical eye. He wasn't handsome in the true sense of being good looking. His features were too harsh for that. He had a wide forehead and a long, narrow nose that looked like it might have been broken at one time.

A thin scar ran across his forehead until it angled down to the corner of his left eye. It was so faint, she would have missed it if she hadn't been lying so close to him. He had a strong, square jaw and thick black eyebrows. A shadow of dark stubble covered his jaw.

His hair was black and was a little on the long side, reaching down past his ears. Tansy was amazed at how large he was. He wasn't fat. She didn't think there was an ounce of fat anywhere on his body. He was just… huge. His shoulders were wide and his chest… damn!

Tansy gulped as she let her eyes run down over his shoulders to his broad chest. There was not a single strand of hair on it. He had muscles on top of muscles. She felt a shudder move through her as feelings she had never felt before flooded her. She wanted him. She wanted him badly. She had never experienced this kind of need before, not even with Branson.

Shit! Tansy thought in dismay. *Where in the hell did this come from? Listen girl, you are not supposed to feel these things. Remember what happened to the last guy you fell for…*

The image of Branson's sightless eyes caused a sharp pain to rush through Tansy and she forced herself to welcome it. She needed to remember that it was too dangerous for her to love someone. Tansy moved silently out from under the covers, ignoring the chill in the air. It was still warmer than the warehouses and abandoned apartment buildings she had been hiding in for the past couple of weeks.

She glanced out the window, noticing it was still dark out. She needed to get dressed, get something to eat, and get out. She turned to look down at the man sleeping in the bed. He rolled toward where she had been. She moved quickly to put her still warm pillow up against him and tuck the covers securely so he wouldn't miss her.

Turning, she grabbed one of the towels that was lying on the floor and wrapped it around her before moving silently out of the room. She made her way to one of the smaller bedrooms she had discovered before she passed out.

She padded over to the armoire and opened it quietly. Inside were several pairs of black jeans, sweaters, and wool jackets. She pulled a small drawer open and found fresh underwear, bras, thick woolen socks, and long-sleeve T-shirts.

The bras were a little on the small size as far as cup wise, so she overflowed a little, but she was happy to have something to wear. The jeans were a little loose around the waist since she had lost weight, but a belt soon corrected that issue. Once she was dressed, she pulled her hair around, quickly brushing and braiding it before tucking it up under one of the black wool caps she found.

She moved back to the bedroom where Mak was still sleeping and picked up her boots. She carried them down the stairs, not bothering to put them on until she was seated in the kitchen. She gave a sigh of relief when she saw her black backpack over in the corner near the door.

"Now, to find some food," she whispered, moving over to the cabinets. She opened several, pulling small packages of crackers, dried soup powder, and power bars out. She stuffed some of it into her backpack while she tore open a power bar and quickly inhaled it. She moved to the refrigerator. Opening it, she found several bottles of water. She opened one and drained it before grabbing the others and stuffing them into her bag.

All that is left is to grab some weapons and I'll be off, Tansy thought, moving over to the pantry where Natasha showed her their stash of weapons.

She lifted out the curved knife she had admired yesterday. Pulling it out of its sheath, she touched the tip, pleased to find it was so sharp that the light pressure broke through her skin. She quickly sheathed it and tucked it into her waistband. She pulled several other small knives out and hid them around her body where they could easily be accessed.

She closed the panel and moved toward the door. She was just about to open it when a feeling she wasn't alone any longer swept through her. Turning, she reacted instinctively, palming a small but deadly knife in her hand.

∽

Strong fingers wrapped around her smaller wrist applying enough pressure she almost dropped the knife. "What in the hell are you doing?" the deep voice growled out.

Tansy's eyes grew wide as she stared up into the flaming silver eyes of a very, very angry alien male. "What does it look like? Do you know how close I came to killing your stupid ass? Don't ever sneak up behind me again," Tansy snapped out, annoyed at the way her body responded to his being so close.

Mak felt the rumble of displeasure as it broke through his pursed lips. When he woke a few minutes ago to discover his mate gone, it had taken every bit of his self-discipline to not over-react. He barely took the time to grab his pants and slide them on before he went in search of her. When he saw her about to leave the farmhouse, fury slid through him. He knew instinctively that she was planning on leaving without him.

He moved closer, trapping her between the door and his body. "Where do you think you are going?"

Tansy's eyes flashed at his obvious attempt to intimidate her. "That is none of your damn business. I have a mission to complete. I appreciate your, Natasha, and Helene's help, but I can handle it from here," she growled back at him.

"You were practically dead yesterday," Mak snapped back. "I do not believe you were handling anything."

Tansy drew in a deep breath and counted to ten slowly. "Listen, I saved your ass, in case you don't remember. I had things under control in that warehouse. I could have made it out," she said pointing her finger into his chest.

"You were unconscious when I removed you from the warehouse, in case *you* don't remember," Mak said, grabbing the hand pressing the finger into his hot flesh and jerking her forward. "If not for me, you would be dead now."

He kept his other hand around the wrist still holding the knife. She was a stubborn little thing. He knew he had applied enough pressure to make her drop it, but she refused to give in.

"What are you doing?" Tansy asked, this time with a hint of unease moving into her voice as she found herself pressed against a hot, smooth wall of flesh.

"I am going to claim you, *je talli*," Mak whispered as he saw the confusion in his mate's dark green eyes. "I am going to make you mine."

"You are?" Tansy breathed out, mesmerized by the hot flames in his dark silver eyes. "I mean, you can't."

"Oh yes I can," Mak said before bending down to cover Tansy's mouth with his own.

Tansy's hand opened and the small thud of the knife hitting the floor was drowned out by the moan that escaped her. She wanted this big ass alien male desperately. She let her hand move up until it tangled in his hair. She was unwilling to take a chance with him pulling away from her. She almost burst out cursing when she felt him pull back until there was barely a breath between them.

"Don't stop," Tansy breathed out against his lips.

"Never have I felt such a feeling before," Mak muttered, bending down and sweeping Tansy up into his arms. "I couldn't stop now even if I wanted to," he admitted softly.

Mak shuddered as he felt Tansy's lips on his neck. She was doing things with her teeth and tongue he had only ever dreamed of a woman doing to him. The feel of the little nips and licks were enough to make him come in his pants. He knew he should take it slow. Before when he was with a female, it would take a long time to build her desire enough for her body to accept his. Even then, he had to use the chemicals in his canines to arouse her. With Tansy, he didn't think he would be able to take the time to ready her, at least not this first time. His body was about ready to explode.

"I should go slowly with you," Mak said hoarsely. "I should prepare your body for mine."

"That's okay. My body has already taken care of the preparing part and I never did like going slow… not much fun," Tansy said, trying to pull his head around to hers so she could taste him again.

"Gods Tansy!" Mak said when he felt her slip her hand down between them so she could reach his straining cock.

"Damn right," Tansy said as he set her down on the bed.

She rolled just far enough to pull the cap off her head. It was quickly followed by her sweater and shirt. Mak was working on her boots and pants. He undid the lacing, before pulling off her boot and sock and tossing both over his broad shoulder. He quickly did the same to the other one. By then, Tansy was panting and cussing up a storm as she tried to unhook the back hooks of the bra she was wearing. She gave a sigh of relief when it finally came undone and she pulled the straps down, tossing it over the side of the bed where it landed on her sweater, shirt and cap.

She gasped when she suddenly felt a large palm between her breasts pushing her back until she lay across the bed with her legs hanging over the side. Mak growled out darkly as he gripped each side of her jeans and pulled. The sound of material tearing was barely louder than the sounds of the pants, gasps, and groans filling the room.

Mak barely had time to push his own pants down to his knees before his body fell on top of Tansy's smaller one. He adjusted his long, hard length against her slick entrance. He felt his canines extending as the mating chemical swept through his body.

He froze as he tried to regain some control over his raging desires. Never had he taken a female like this before. He fought with the shame at losing so much control. His breathing was labored as he battled to win the fight not to frighten the tiny figure trapped under him.

A fierce shudder went through him as his cock brushed against the soft curls lying in the vee between Tansy's sweet, long legs. He thought he just about had himself back under control when he felt the sweet touch of Tansy's tongue as it ran up the length of one of his canines.

"Oh Gods!" Mak cried out as his body thrust forward in reaction to the explosion of overwhelming need at the sensual act.

∾

Tansy was on fire from the first touch when he grabbed her wrist to stop her from stabbing him to the moment he pulled her against all that hot, delicious flesh. All she could think about was touching and tasting every tantalizing inch of him. She was beyond thinking rationally. For the first time in her life, she wanted something for herself so badly, so desperately she was willing to reach out and grab it.

When he had pushed her back to grip her pants, she never expected him to literally rip them off her. She had been stunned at his strength. Hell, she knew he was strong, but she never realized he was that damn strong.

Her heart was pounding when she looked at him and saw his dazed, passion-filled face. There was no denying he wanted her. Her eyes widened as she saw his teeth extending. She vaguely remembered them being that way in the warehouse but she had thought it was her imagination.

Now, the sight of them only re-enforced that this male was not from her world. Tansy half thought she should be afraid, but if anything, the picture of his flaming eyes, extended teeth, and huge muscles straining did the exact opposite. They made her feel safe, desired... loved. The moment his body covered hers, she moved to run her tongue along one of the extended canines, wanting to feel and taste him in the most primitive, basic way. She wanted him to lose control and take her as she had never been taken before.

She focused on pulling him down to her. When he closed his eyes, she feared he would pull away, stop, or just as bad, slow down. Tansy shifted her body until she could feel his hard, swollen cock against her hot vaginal opening. She wound one arm around his head, pulling him closer, while the other slid under his arm to grip his back. She raised her legs to wrap around his huge thighs. This position helped to raise her up until they were aligned.

She was breathing fast at the first touch, nervous as to whether she would be able to handle his thick cock. She felt like she was going to burst into flames if she didn't feel him deep inside her soon. Reaching up, she ran the tip of her tongue up the length of his extended canine. What happened next shocked her.

"Oh Gods!" Mak's thick voice exploded as his body jerked forward, impaling her smaller form on him.

Tansy gasped at the sudden intrusion. Even as slick as she was, it was a shock to feel him suddenly buried balls deep inside her. Tears burned her eyes at the sudden burst of pain but it faded just as quickly as her body adjusted to the steel of his cock.

She wrapped her arms tighter around him and used her heels to let him know she wanted him to move as she began to rock back and forth in the ageless dance of mating. She felt every inch of him as he pulled out and pushed in. Each move slid over sensitive nerves increasing the slickness of her vaginal channel until there was no way of knowing where he began and she ended. They were forged together into one being.

You feel so good. I don't ever want you to stop, Tansy thought in a delicious haze.

I will always be with you, Mak responded as another shudder swept through his body as she clenched him even tighter. *Gods Tansy, this is incredible.*

Tansy stopped thinking as Mak began moving faster and harder until all she could do was hang on tightly as he rocked into her body over and over. He nudged her head to the side, bending over her and wrapping his arms around her to pull her even closer. Tansy leaned into him, biting down on his shoulder as her body began to shake with the need for release. She fought against it, not wanting this time to end. Her body shattered into convulsions of ecstasy when he sank his teeth into her shoulder.

Tansy's body arched and a small scream tore from her throat as her climax exploded outward in wave after wave of pure pleasure. Mak refused to stop even when she hoarsely cried out as tiny aftershocks rocked her. He slammed into her harder and deeper than she thought possible.

His huge body tensed before he jerked his mouth away from her hot flesh and roared out his own release. Tremors racked his body as he released his seed deep inside her. Tansy could feel the heat of it as it poured into her womb. It was almost like even that part of him was claiming her, possessing her until she was no longer just Tansy Bell.

Tansy looked up at the man caging her under him in confusion and worry. He tugged at a part of her that she thought she had lost a long time ago... her heart. The thought of anything bad happening to him because of her sent such deep waves of pain through her, she was surprised she didn't cry out from the agony. Raising trembling hands to touch his face, she ran her fingers tenderly over the rugged planes, trying to memorize them.

Mak buried his face into Tansy's shoulder where he had bitten her. He gently brushed the tip of his tongue over the mark, smiling when he felt her shiver in response. Now he understood why his brother J'kar was so protective of his mate.

He also understood why his mother had the glow about her and his father's strange, satisfied expression all the time now. If this is what it was like to not only have a bond mate, but one that was as passionate as his was, he could see himself walking around with a smile of his own.

"*Ta me ja'te, je talli.* I love you, my heart," Mak whispered against Tansy's skin.

I love you, too, Tansy thought, quietly wrapping her arms around his waist and pulling him closer.

CHAPTER TEN

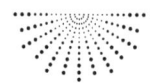

Mak glanced at Tansy. She had been unusually quiet since they had mated the second time in the bathing room. After their first round of love-making, he had picked her up and taken her to the bathing room to clean her. She had nuzzled against him quietly.

He thought to just bathe and care for her. He cursed when he saw all the fading bruises on her and a few new ones from him. Determined to care for her properly, he had turned the water to as hot as she could stand and picked up a small cloth and a bar of soap where he proceeded to gently wash every inch of her delicate skin. He paused at the sealant patch. Gently removing it, he chuckled at her exclamation of surprise to see the skin completely healed with only a small pink scar.

"How?" Tansy started to say before just shaking her head. "Thank you."

"It is my pleasure to care for you," Mak murmured as he ran the cloth up the inside of her leg.

Tansy's hands fell to his shoulders and she began kneading them as he continued to clean her. Soon, it was her turn to wash him. When she went to her knees in front of him, he fought to keep his cock from swelling at the erotic sight of her kneeling before him. He forced himself to stare straight ahead so he would not upset her with the fact that he wanted her again.

His breath exploded out of him and he found he had to hang onto the long bar above the shower for support when she suddenly wrapped her lips around his hard length and began sucking on him. His eyes widened in disbelief before almost closing in ecstasy at the vision of her beautiful lips bringing him to untold pleasure. He flushed as he remembered how quickly he had found release again and again.

"What is worrying you?" Mak asked, coming up behind her where he rested his hands on her slender hips.

Tansy looked over her shoulder at Mak with a frown before turning back around to focus on the rice she was cooking. They were having a strange breakfast of fish, yellow rice, and steamed vegetables. Since Natasha and Helene did not stay here often and were not planning for their visit, the only things available were boxed, canned, or frozen.

"It's not safe for you to be near me. I've been thinking about my assignment. From the very beginning I had a bad feeling about it. The only reason I accepted it was because it was a chance to erase Boris Avilov. But, there was something that just didn't feel right," Tansy's voice faded away as she looked out the window at the Maral deer feeding. There were four of them outside now, a stag and three females.

"Why?" Mak asked, moving next to her so he could lean against the counter and see her face as she spoke.

He was discovering she had many secrets that she kept hidden deep inside her. He could see them in her eyes. One of those secrets was how she remained untouched. He knew from the little he had talked with Tink that females from this world were not protected by the men within their family group as the Prime females were. He had even seen the holovid of Tink's description of what Tansy did to him in the bathing room. He did not think such a thing was possible, but he had been very, very wrong. It was not only possible but if he had any say in the matter, it would be repeated many, many times. He wanted her to share her secrets. Perhaps then, the dark shadows in them would fade.

He leaned over and brushed a thick strand of hair back from her face that had come loose from where she had braided it after their bath. "Why do you feel this?" he asked again.

Tansy released her breath and focused back on the rice, stirring it slowly. "I usually work for Ted Rogers. I have since I started in the program. He is my exclusive handler. No one else is supposed to know who I am, where I am at, nothing. I am a ghost in the system. I take my assignments from him and I report what happens to him. I received this assignment from his boss, Craig Knapp. Craig is an arrogant pretty boy. He sits on the committees, he looks good in the press, he talks the talk to the politicians but he doesn't dirty his hands with those of us known as expendable. He wanted to meet with me to give me the dossier on this assignment but I refused. It is out of protocol and there are some things I won't do even for Ted. Instead there was a drop. I cased the area thoroughly because I was getting really bad vibes from it," Tansy said, glancing at Mak before reaching around him to get a bowl for the rice.

Mak placed his hand on her arm to stop her. "Why did you not talk to this Ted Rogers about your feelings?"

"I tried but I couldn't reach him. That was another red flag. I've never had a problem reaching Ted if I needed him. It is his job to always be there if I call. I found out right before this assignment went to hell his daughter had been in a car accident," Tansy said, grabbing the bowl. "Only I don't think it was an accident. I think they wanted Ted out of the way and the only way to do that was to strike at his daughter. She is the only thing in this world that means more to him than his job."

"Why would this man, this Craig Knapp, want to harm you? Are you not fighting for the same thing?" Mak asked quietly as he pulled the fish out of the oven and set it on the table next to the rice and plates.

"You would think so but I started doing a little digging using some unconventional help," Tansy said with a small smirk.

"RITA?" Mak asked with a grin.

Tansy nodded. "RITA. I guess you met her, sort of?"

Mak laughed. "Yes. She not only invaded my brother's warship after your sister Tink found herself aboard it, but she has become a fixture at the palace. She likes to get into our computer systems and 'tweak' them as she says."

"Oh God!" Tansy moaned. "Thank goodness you don't have my mom and dad there. If you did, your world would never be the same. I've never met two hornier people in my life," she groaned out with a shake of her head.

"Well..." Mak chuckled as he came up behind her and bent her over the chair so he could rub the front his pants against her. His chuckle turned to a deep throated laugh as he saw her blush at the feel of his cock straining against the front again. "I am not so sure they are the horniest two people on my world anymore. Your mother has been instructing the women of my world on how to not only please their bond mates but what their bond mates can do to please them."

Tansy turned in Mak's arms with a horrified gasp. "You have *my* mom... on *your* world?" she squeaked out. "Do you have any idea what she can do? Do you have any idea..."

Mak sealed his mouth over hers in a deep kiss. "Yes, I know. She and your father have already corrupted my father who is the leader of our clans. She is needed. Your sister Tink is breeding something called twins and insisted she needed your mother with her during this time."

"Twins!" Tansy echoed in shock before smiling brightly up at Mak. "Tink's having twins?! I'm going to be an aunt!"

Mak's eyes blazed with desire as Tansy's face was transformed at the news of her younger sister's breeding. He wondered if she would be as happy if he were to plant his seed in her womb. The desire to see her swelling with their younglings was almost overwhelming. He wanted to see her rounded and glowing like her sister. He had released the mating chemical into her this morning at least twice, once the first time they mated and again in the bathing room when he took her in the shower. He knew it would normally take several tries before she would become fertile but even Terra was not sure how the mating chemical would work on this species.

Mak cursed as he fought to think rationally. He needed to get her to safety before they even thought of breeding. This was no place for his mate. She was still tired, even if she refused to admit it, and she definitely needed to be fed regularly. He was not a very good mate at all if he didn't make sure she was safe, happy, and healthy first.

"Sit, eat, and finish telling me what happened," Mak instructed as he poured them each a glass of water to go with their meal.

"Well, I went to the drop, but I didn't pick it up. I cased the area pretty damn good and almost missed the assassin sent to take me out. He was good," Tansy said with a small smile. "But I was better."

Mak laughed at the bloodthirsty gleam in Tansy's eyes. "You 'erased' him?" Mak asked with a chuckle.

Tansy shook her head. "No, I knew the guy. He had been told I was a double agent. Let's just say we had a heart to heart. It is one thing to erase someone you know is an infection to the world; it is another to erase one of the good guys using a good guy. He simply delivered a message to Knapp. If he fucked with me again, I would erase his ass."

"What did this Knapp do?" Mak asked darkly, thinking if Tansy didn't kill him then Mak would not have a problem doing it.

"He denied it, of course. He accused some lesser office junky of wanting to take his place and make him look bad. He is just an asshole to think I would believe that since not even he should have known about me," Tansy snorted as she took a bite of her fish.

"Damn, but I'm a good cook sometimes," she moaned as it hit her stomach. "Enough about me, though, I want to hear about you. Tell me about your world."

Over the next hour, Mak described his home world to Tansy. He talked about his home in the mountains away from the city and the palace. He told her about some of the different worlds he had traveled to and the different species who inhabited those worlds. He explained how some were humanoid like the Prime and those from Earth and how others were not.

Throughout the meal they laughed and joked. He liked seeing this side of Tansy. She was relaxed and the dark shadows in her eyes lightened at his tales of his and his brothers' adventures as they were growing up. He talked about some of the different clans and the problems they had finding females who could be their bond mates. They had just finished cleaning the kitchen when the satellite phone in Mak's pocket vibrated.

"Speak," Mak said, opening the phone.

"You and Tansy need to get out of there immediately," Helene's quiet voice came over the phone. "Take the Land Rover through the trail in the woods. It will take you over the mountain. There is a cave hidden in the side of the mountain just to the north of the fork in the road. Leave the Land Rover off to the side of the road and take the vehicle in the cave. Head north toward Ramenskoe; it is a little over 50 km from there. Natasha and I will meet you there. There is a small pub called Krylom. I have to go."

Mak smothered a curse as he glanced at Tansy's blank face. She was trying to shut him out. He slipped the satellite phone back in his pocket and reached for her hand, frowning at her when she pulled back a step.

"What is it?" she asked tightly.

"Helene says we need to leave immediately," Mak replied tersely.

Tansy nodded, pulling on her jacket over the sweater she was wearing. She pulled the dark cap out of the pocket of the jacket where she had stuck it earlier and quickly pulled her hair up into a bun and covered it. She walked over to the pantry. Pulling the hidden panel open, she grabbed several automatic pistols, an MT116 sniper rifle, and an AEK918G. She took several boxes of ammo as well before closing the panel. She turned just as Mak came back into the room, strapping on a cross belt over his chest. He frowned when he saw the stag suddenly lurch into action and take off, followed by the females. His mouth tightened.

"Get to the transport. I will follow you shortly," he snarled in a low dangerous voice.

Tansy's mouth flattened out. "Don't get your ass killed. I'll be really pissed at you if you do," she said quietly before turning on her heel and moving to the door leading to the basement.

Mak's smile turned from tender to savage. He would not be the one dying. He moved over to the window and peered out at the dark shapes.

He had no problems seeing in the dimmer light of the woods. He moved into the living area and up the stairs. He would not wait for them to come to him.

CHAPTER ELEVEN

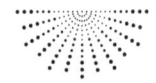

Tansy fought the urge to turn around and charge out of the house, guns blazing. She would do anything to protect the huge alien male who had captured her heart. She hadn't admitted to him out loud that she loved his stupid, arrogant, ornery ass, but he had heard her thoughts. She froze as she moved through the narrow tunnel lit only by a connected series of rope lighting. Their link…

Shit a gold brick! Tansy thought as it occurred to her they could use their link to take the sons-of-bitches out.

That seems like a very painful thing to do. I am not sure it is even possible, Mak's serious reply sounded in her mind.

What do you think isn't possible? Tansy asked in confusion as she walked toward the trap door in the shed.

'Shitting a gold brick'. I do not think such as thing is physically possible, even for someone as large as myself, came the calm reply.

Tansy bit her lip to keep from laughing out loud. He was going to get them both killed if he came up with comments like that at times like this. She was about to tell him that it was just an expression when his silent laugh echoed through her mind letting her know he had understood her meaning.

And the answer to your thoughts is 'no'. I will not allow you to put your-

self in danger. Stay out of sight until I can join you, Mak's determined order came through loud and clear.

I seem to remember telling you I don't take orders from anyone... ever. I'm going to circle around behind them, Tansy replied just as calmly as he had a moment ago. *I'll meet you in the middle.*

I am going to whip your ass if you do, Mak growled out. *You will do what I tell you.*

Tansy chuckled before replying. *Before you think of whipping my ass, may I remind you that you will have to go to sleep sometime in your life and I will be ready for that day.*

Fine! But don't think I won't tell your mother what you are doing! Mak threatened in a dark voice.

You wouldn't dare! Tansy hissed back, but her footsteps slowed as she neared the end of the tunnel. *Mak? You wouldn't, would you? Not really? Mak? MAK!*

Mak didn't answer. He knew deep down that Tansy would do anything to spare her mother and father any grief. He was not above using that threat and following through with it if it kept her safe. She didn't realize she was still weak from blood loss, was not thinking clearly from lack of sleep, and still run down from not having enough to eat for too long a period of time.

He had seen the same thing in warriors back home during a time when their people had been at war. He had watched too many warriors fall to lesser adversaries because they had not had time or not stopped to regain their strength before entering a battle. He would not watch the same thing happen to his mate when he was able to prevent it.

You don't fight fair, Tansy's soft voice came through in reproach. *But, I know you are right. I would be a liability right now, not an asset. Please be careful... for me.*

Mak's heart melted at the hesitant request at the end. He could feel the fear and pain behind the words. It wasn't what she said but what she didn't that he heard. She had lost someone she cared about before. It was that someone, who put the shadows in her eyes.

Branson, Tansy's soft voice whispered before it faded away.

Mak slipped into the master bedroom and moved toward the window that overlooked the front of the house. He watched from behind the curtains as two men came up out of the woods along the drive toward the front porch. He waited until he was sure they couldn't see him before he quietly opened the window and stepped through it onto the roof over the porch.

He crept silently down the slope of the roof, waiting patiently as the men came up under him. He pulled his two short swords from the sheaths on his back, gripping them tightly. He would only have one chance to take them out without alerting the other men coming up in the woods behind the wood frame house. With practiced ease, he dropped down behind the men before they could even step up onto the porch, slicing through their backs into their hearts, killing them instantly. He turned and sprinted for the woods before the bodies even had a chance to hit the ground.

He had counted four separate shadows in the woods behind the house, but suspected there might be more hidden. He focused for a split second on Tansy, making sure she was where she promised she would be. He did not want to take a chance of her being found.

I'm fine. Stay focused on what you are doing and don't you dare shut me out or I will be the one doing the ass whipping, came her calm voice.

Mak bit back a grin that his mate would even dare to think of whipping him. He marveled at the fact she was so different from all the other females he had known. She was smaller, more fragile in many ways, but yet seemed stronger and fearless in others.

I'll show you fearless if you start thinking of other women, Tansy growled back. *Now keep your head in the fucking game. I wasn't kidding about being pissed if you got hurt.*

Has anyone ever told you that you are very bossy? Mak asked as he moved into the darker shadows of the woods.

Bite me! Tansy snapped back.

With pleasure, Mak murmured as he entered the woods.

He knelt down, glancing around him as his eyes adjusted to the dimmer light. He listened carefully. There to the right, the slight sound of leaves being crushed. He rose and took off through the woods moving with the speed and skill of a Prime Warrior. He could see the shadow moving to the left of him. Jumping, he grabbed the branch of a tree about ten feet up and swung up, landing on the thick limb with ease.

I can do that, Tansy murmured softly in his head.

There will be no need for you to have to once I get you to my home, Mak growled back darkly.

~

Tansy pulled back until she was just a shadow in Mak's mind. She would follow along with him in case he needed some assistance, but she would not distract him. A shiver went through her at the dark promise in his voice. It disturbed her.

She would cherish the time she had with him, but there could never be anything permanent. His life was back in his world and hers was here. She had been thinking about her current assignment. Not all of the pieces were clear yet, but the picture was beginning to form. She had been sold out. The only thing she needed to know was how far up the sale had gone. The first place she was going to start looking was back in Washington. A visit with Craig Knapp was in order. Perhaps it was time for Craig to discover just how well the government trained their operatives.

She refused to think of Mak's promise right now. She would return him safely to Cosmos' warehouse where he could travel back to his world through whatever in the hell Cosmos built. Then, she would shut it down. It was too dangerous for something like that to exist. If one world could be accessed, then so could another. As much as it tore her up at the thought of never seeing Mak again, she knew it was the only choice.

Tansy climbed the narrow wooden ladder at the end of the tunnel. According to Natasha, it would come up under the Land Rover. Natasha said they designed it that way so it was hidden. Unless someone was down on their hands and knees looking under the vehicle they wouldn't see anyone. In addition, it gave them the advantage of seeing if anyone was in the garage.

She quietly slid the well-lubricated bolt to the side, unlocking the trap door. Lowering it just enough so she could stick her head up through the opening, she cautiously glanced around. She didn't see or hear anything.

Pulling herself up, she rolled over and lay on her back, a Makarov pistol in each hand. She waited patiently before tucking her arms against her side and rolling out from under the vehicle. She came up on one knee with her back protected. The garage had two windows, one on each side. They were small, no more than two foot by two foot, but let in enough light so she didn't have any trouble seeing.

Tansy rose, slowly circling so she could get a good feel for any possible places someone could hide. She glanced up at the ceiling, noting there was nothing but open tresses. The garage was empty except for the Land Rover. It was an older model with a winch on the front and a re-enforced bar across the back. If anyone tried to ram them, their vehicle would suffer more damage than the Land Rover.

Tansy tucked one of the pistols in the waistband of her jeans and quietly opened the door of the SUV. She reached up under the driver's seat, feeling around for the plastic bag containing the key. A small smile curved her lips when she found it. She gripped it tightly in her hand and stood up.

She was about to climb into the Land Rover when a shadow passed by the window. She immediately closed the driver's door and crouched down low. Crab-walking over to the window, she stood up once she was against the wall. A second shadow passed by.

~

"We are to check the garage," a low voice whispered in Russian. "Rurik and Savin should be ready to enter through the front. Osip, Pasha, Vanya and Yegor will take the back. You and I are to make sure she does not have any transportation. Then, we are to cover the sides. Osip said the Baskov sisters were in a transport van and their vehicle was left outside of security headquarters. Sip's informant did not see anyone get in the vehicle with them, but Osip says the female has connections to the sisters."

"How is it possible the female could kill so many of our men at the warehouse?" the second voice asked gruffly. "I heard she was injured. Blood was found on the wall where one of Avilov's guards shot her. Karp had run her to ground. You know what a mean bastard he was. He made sure she could not stay anywhere long enough to rest or heal. She must have had some help."

"If she does, we will take whoever is helping her out. Just remember, Avilov wants her alive. She doesn't have to be in good shape, but she does have to be alive. He plans on making sure she embraces death when he finally kills her. I heard he is going to kill her family first. He has already sent men to take care of this Cosmos who also has connections to the sisters. He will take the sisters out as well to show those in the politsia that he means business," the man said.

"You two need to shut up!" a third voice whispered angrily. "Get in position, now!"

∽

Tansy moved back, looking around. There was no place to hide. She would need to take them out quickly and quietly. She pushed the gun in her hand into her backpack.

She moved silently over to the Land Rover, opened the driver's door and set the backpack behind the passenger seat before closing and locking the door again quietly. There really wasn't a good place to hide except either in the Land Rover or back in the tunnel. It looked like the tunnel was going to win if the men were persistent in getting into the garage.

There was a heavy bar across the outside of the double doors with a heavy duty padlock on it. It would be no problem for the Land Rover to break through. If she was lucky, the men would think it was secure and no one could get in.

Tansy looked at the two windows again to make sure it was clear. She was just about to crawl back under the SUV when a slight sliver of light caught her attention. A grin lit up Tansy's face when she saw the small hidden door against the wall where an empty workbench stood. If she hadn't gotten low enough, she would have missed it.

Natasha and Helene were two very clever women, Tansy thought as she changed directions.

She laid down on the bottom part of the bench and rolled through the opening, landing outside of the garage behind a set of well-placed barrels. She was still hidden but now she was outside and behind the men. From her count, there were eight men total. She would take out the two here, Mak already took out two so that left four. She could handle that.

You are not to handle anything! Mak's deep voice bit out. *You were to stay hidden.*

Yeah well, they found my hiding spot, Tansy replied hotly. *Focus on the guys near you. I can handle these two.*

You are making me very angry, Mak snarled.

Tansy barely suppressed the chuckle building up inside her. *You might as well get used to it. I have that effect on people.*

∽

Mak pursed his lips to keep the roar of rage from escaping. He remained frozen on the branch, none of his internal fury evident in the stillness of his body. The only way anyone would know he was upset was if they were to look into his eyes. Dark, silver flames burned with deadly intent. These men had come to harm his mate. He would kill all of them without mercy.

Mak waited until the figure was just past the branch he was on before he dropped down behind him. He grabbed the man by the neck and slammed him up against the trunk of the tree. He squeezed his hand just enough to keep the man from making any noise.

Reaching into his vest pocket, he pulled the translator out and pressed it against the man's temple. "How many men?"

"Fuck you," the man choked out when Mak loosened his hold just enough to let the man speak.

"Wrong answer," Mak said and squeezed his fingers, crushing the man's throat.

Mak slid the translator back into his vest pocket and let the man drop to the ground. He noted the man was still alive, but he wouldn't be for long if the blue tint to his skin was any indication. He reached down and removed the weapons from the man and picked up the assault rifle the man dropped when he grabbed him.

Rising, he tilted his head to the side and listened carefully as his eyes scanned the shadowed woods. He began moving again when he didn't hear anything. He kept to the shadows as much as possible, making a loop so he would come up behind any additional men.

Mak? Tansy's soft voice called out in his mind.

Yes, je talli? Mak responded in a cool tone.

I counted eight men. If you have taken out three, then that leaves five. I'll stay hidden as long as possible. There are two men at the garage. The others are heading for the back of the house. They are not sure I am here, or if I am, whether or not I am alone, Tansy said quietly. *They plan to kill my family and Natasha and Helene. I overheard two of the men say they have sent men to kill Cosmos.*

Mak bit back a curse. If Cosmos was in danger then that meant Terra was in danger. He was ready to be done with this world! They would need to warn Cosmos to leave.

It would be best if he returned to Baade with Terra. Their father would accept Cosmos as Terra's mate. He would have no choice. At least there, he would know his sister was safe.

I am coming for you, Mak bit out harshly.

CHAPTER TWELVE

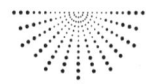

Mak made his way up behind the garage. He stopped at the outer rim of the woods, standing at an angle so his body was mostly hidden from view. He could see three other men fanning out behind the house. That meant two men were not visible. He was about to move forward when the bark next to him flew out in all directions. He whirled around, running back into the woods as fast as he could. Within moments, he was to the east of them.

He could hear them yelling now. One of the men near Tansy had spotted him and fired. He let out a roar when he heard Tansy return fire on the man. Loud curses could be heard as the men scrambled for cover.

"Bitch!" the man who fired on Mak called out hoarsely. "Kill her! I don't care what Avilov said, kill her!"

"Shut up, Viktor!" Osip yelled. "Do not kill her! I repeat, do not kill her. Wound her."

Pasha raised his rifle and looked through the scope. "There is something else out there," he yelled out.

Cursing, he wiped a hand across his eyes. Either his vision was suddenly blurry or whatever was out there was moving faster than he could eye clearly. He tried to gauge where it was going, but by the time he tried to focus, the image was gone.

"Osip, there is something the hell out there!" Pasha yelled out again.

"What the hell do you mean something? Shoot the bastard!" Osip shouted back. "Vanya, Yegor cover Luka."

Pasha moved slightly. There, the figure of a… Pasha felt the shiver of ice clear to his soul. Whatever in the hell it was, it was not human. It was too damn big, too damn fast to be human. The figure moved with lightning speed toward the garage where the gunfire had come from just a few moments before. He aimed carefully and pulled the trigger.

The figure didn't even slow down. He was sure he had hit him. Before he could aim again, the figure disappeared. A hoarse scream filled the air before Viktor's lifeless body was tossed out into the yard, his arms and neck at a strange angle.

"Luka! Where are you?" Osip shouted out from behind a small wooden fence. "Luka!"

∼

Tansy lowered the body of the one called Luka down to the ground. She had surprised him as he came around the corner of the garage at the same time Mak was turning the one called Viktor into a human pretzel. She had made quick work of disposing of him with the sharp curved knife Natasha had shown her the day before.

She had no choice, but to take Luka out. He had been getting into position to shoot at Mak. She was hoping to keep at least one of the assholes alive long enough to find out what Avilov's plans were.

At the rate Mak is taking them out, I won't have anything but corpses, and they just don't talk, no matter how much I try to get them to, Tansy thought in frustration.

Tansy gave in to the desire to look around. She had heard the sound of a high power rifle and feared Mak might have been hit. It was only the fact that Viktor was tossed like a discarded toy after the shot that gave her hope the shot had missed him.

She tried to touch his mind, but he had closed her off. The lack of contact both stunned and pissed her off. She was stunned at how empty she felt without his presence and pissed that she was letting him inside the carefully built barriers she had built around her.

Hell, it was like a fucking black hole, Tansy thought in aggravation at the desolate emptiness.

It wasn't like she should even give a damn. What they had was a brief interlude under a stressful situation. It didn't really mean anything. She sure as heck shouldn't be ready to cry like a baby because he had blocked her out. It just proved if he could lock her out so easily, then he didn't really give a damn about her. Tansy ignored the shaft of pain the thought caused and focused on the relief that it would be easier to say goodbye when the time came.

Satisfied with her reasoning, she decided she was done with sitting back and waiting for the Calvary to rescue her. This was her assignment. She needed to get it back under her control. She had to get to Ramenskoe, get Helene and Natasha into a safe house, get to Cosmos and kill the bastards sent after him, then clean house in Washington. She didn't have time to pussyfoot around with Avilov's lackeys or an alien male who wanted to play house.

Pulling the pistol from the waistband of her jeans, she checked the clip and was satisfied she had enough rounds to deal with the remaining men. Tansy peeked around the corner of the garage trying to gauge where the men were hiding. She still didn't see where Mak was. This was the side that Viktor had been on so he should be somewhere close by.

Tansy moved along the side of the building, keeping her eyes focused for any movement. There were two smaller sheds about ten meters to the left. Tansy stopped at the corner and looked around. Her eyes widened as she followed a small trail of blood leading to the closest shed. It could only mean one thing… Mak had been hit.

~

Mak ignored the blood soaking his side. The bullet had grazed him, cutting a clean path just below his ribcage. He focused on the remaining men. There were four left.

Mak was tired of the games. He pulled a couple of the small charges he had attached to the leather straps that crisscrossed the front of his vest. The small silver balls, no bigger than a small button, held a powerful explosive. Mak palmed three of them in his hand. He rolled his shoulders before sprinting out from behind the shed at a fast run. Tossing the small explosive balls with deadly precision at the targets, he tucked and rolled as the men opened fire at the same time as the explosives hit their target.

The explosions shook the ground. Where the man behind the fencing used to be was a deep hole. Nothing remained of the man called Osip, not even small body parts. The same fate belonged to Vanya who had hidden behind an old wagon. Pasha was trapped under the wreckage of the collapsed roof of the porch. A beam lay across his legs, trapping him. His rifle, which had been ripped out of his hands by the explosion, lay too far for him to reach. He tried to get to his pistol, but every movement sent excruciating pain through him.

Mak walked up to where the man was pinned on the porch and knelt down. Mak quickly searched the trapped figure for weapons, removing them and tossing them into the yard. He pressed the translator against the man's temple. He needed to know how many others were a threat to his mate and his family.

"How many others?" he growled out.

∼

Pasha looked in fear at the face of a man who was not human. The male's face was set in a cold mask of rage. His eyes were burning silver flames of fury that promised Pasha he would not die easily. It was the male's mouth that held Pasha frozen in terror, unable to speak at first.

Long canines extended down in sharp points, each end held a drop of liquid that held him mesmerized. There was no way this could have been faked. When the man pressed the device against his temple, he thought for sure it was a type of weapon. He breathed a sigh of relief when he realized he could understand what the man was saying.

Pasha watched as the man drew a deadly looking short sword from the leather sheath on his back. "There were eight of us," Pasha said desperately. "Eight of us were sent to bring the female back."

Mak looked down into the terror-filled eyes coldly. "I have killed five. Where are the other two?"

Pasha shook his head. "I don't know," he answered hoarsely. "I wasn't keeping an eye on them. They should be here somewhere unless they took off."

Mak looked down at the trapped man dispassionately. "I will let you live so you may give the man who wants to harm my mate and her family a message. Tell him I am coming for him. I will kill any who stand in my way." Mak stood up. "You will give him this message. If I ever see you again, I will slice you into small pieces very, very slowly. You understand me?" Mak asked coldly.

Pasha nodded desperately. Money was of no use to him if he was dead and he had no doubt he would be dead if he ever crossed this man's path again. This huge male frightened him more than Boris Avilov ever could. He also knew that Avilov's time on Earth was about to end very soon. He would deliver the message, not in person, but he would deliver the message and then he would disappear.

Mak turned away from where Pasha was lying and started walking across the yard. He was concerned with the disappearance of the other males. He needed to find his mate and make sure she was safe. He had cut her off for two reasons: first, he was upset with her for not staying in the tunnel where he knew she would have been safe, and second, he didn't want her to know he had been hurt. He knew she would have come charging out with the mistaken idea of saving his ass.

His eyes lit up with fury when he saw her coming out from around the side of the garage. She had a pistol in one hand and a bloody knife in the other. He strode toward her and grabbed the hand holding the knife. He raised it up and looked at her sternly.

"What?" Tansy asked. "He fell on it," she joked.

"You were supposed to stay hidden!" Mak growled out in a low, frustrated voice.

"Yeah, and you weren't supposed to get hurt," Tansy replied with a raised eyebrow. "It looks like you listen about as good as I do," she added before turning away from him.

Mak raised his hands as if he wanted to wrap them around her neck and strangle her. Tansy looked over her shoulder, catching him in the act and grinned in amusement. She was about to make a smart-ass comment when movement out of the corner of her eye pulled a curse out of her instead. She stepped in front of Mak's huge frame and fired at the same time as the hidden figure did.

Tansy felt the burning fire of the bullet as it hit her in the shoulder, causing her to jerk backwards into Mak's hard body. Everything seemed to slow down after that. She watched as a nice little hole opened up between the man's eyes before he collapsed.

She felt Mak's arms wrap around her falling body and his roar of rage before she was gently lowered to the ground. Everything seemed to accelerate to fast forward the moment she was lying flat on the hard ground. Pain exploded through her as Mak ripped the material of her jacket and shirt apart to see how badly she was hit.

Yup, Tansy thought as black spots began appearing before her eyes, *getting shot really sucked.*

∼

"You already said that," Tansy groaned again. "I know you are mad at me. Enough already! I haven't had my ass chewed this bad since... ever! Even my mom and dad don't harp as much as you do," Tansy complained as she shifted in the seat of the SUV trying to get comfortable.

"Harp! Harp!" Mak sputtered in aggravation. "You are impossible! How do you expect me to protect you if you do not listen to me? You are small, delicate, fragile, and need to learn how to be more obedient!"

"Like that is ever likely to happen," Tansy muttered under her breath as she looked out the passenger side window.

After she was shot Mak had done his Mojo with the little MED kit he had. She was definitely going to have to invest in a couple of cases of the medical kits before she closed down the gateway Cosmos opened. The pain patch was some wickedly powerful shit. She didn't feel him pulling the bullet out at all and the HM mist and sealant patch...they were pure magic as far as Tansy was concerned. A quick trip into the house afterwards for a new shirt and jacket, another one to ask Pasha a few more questions and they were on the back road heading for the cave and the other vehicle Natasha and Helene had stashed.

The pain patch was a blessing as the road wasn't the smoothest. Neither was Mak's driving, but Tansy didn't think it was in her best interest to say anything. For the last hour, Mak had driven at a brutal pace over the rough road, taking his anger and frustration out of the poor SUV's suspension.

Thirty minutes into the journey, he had started in on her. She was forced to listen to him chew her out for doing such a dangerous job, not being careful, not listening, not taking care of herself, not... blah, blah, blah. After about five minutes she tuned him out. It was either that or jump out of the rapidly moving SUV. The only thing that stopped her from doing that was it would prove him right because she would probably end up with a broken neck at the rate he was driving.

"Are you even listening to me?" Mak demanded.

Tansy flushed when she realized he had asked her the same question three times. "No," she replied with a pout as she wiggled in her seat again.

Mak glanced at her briefly before drawing in a deep breath and releasing it. "Is that no, you are not in pain or no, you are not listening to me?" he asked in a quieter voice.

Tansy smiled sheepishly. "No, I wasn't listening to you. But, if it helps, I'm not in any pain either."

Mak couldn't stop the chuckle that escaped at her answer. At least he didn't have to worry about whether she would be truthful with him. He had finally worked through the anger and fear that had held him in its grip since she was hurt.

He was angry at not doing a better job of protecting her. He knew there was another threat, but all thought had deserted him when he saw her walking toward him with the bloody knife. He needed to know the blood was not hers.

His fear when she stepped in front of him had been indescribable. His heart actually stopped for the briefest moment when he felt her jerk back against him and he smelled her rich blood. He feared, at first, the injury had been a wound he could not heal. That was one reason he had been less than gentle when he tore her jacket and shirt from her body.

"You will tell me if you feel any pain," Mak said gruffly.

"I will," Tansy replied softly. She leaned forward when she saw the fork in the road. "There's the fork. Helene said the cave was to the north."

Mak slowed down, taking the left branch of the fork. A short ways down there was a small logging road off to the side. He pulled into it. The Land Rover would be hidden from the air and not easily seen unless someone drove down the road. Pulling to a stop, he shut off the engine and turned toward Tansy. He wrapped his huge hand around the back of her neck and pulled her forward until he could crush her lips with his in a hard, fierce kiss.

"Do not ever put yourself in front of me again," Mak said before he released her and opened the door.

Tansy watched as he unfolded his huge body from the SUV. Shaking her head to clear it, she opened the passenger side door and jumped out. She bit back a grimace of discomfort at the sudden movement.

She glanced over at Mak to see if he noticed. The dark scowl on his face said he had. Tansy rolled her eyes and moved to the back passenger door to get her backpack. She needed to call Cosmos.

Dammit, Tansy thought crossly, *you are getting careless, girl. Get your act together before you get yourself killed.*

Getting killed is not an option, Mak growled out in her mind.

It's not like I have it marked on my calendar, damn it! And, get out of my head. You aren't allowed into it unless I invite you and I'm still pissed at you for shutting me out earlier so get lost! Tansy growled back in annoyance.

Tansy pulled the satellite phone out of her backpack and powered it on. After entering the passcode, she waited impatiently for RITA to pick up as she began following Mak up the logging road to the base of the mountain. She needed to warn Cosmos to expect company.

"Tansy?" Cosmos' voice came on over the phone anxiously.

"Hey, Cosmos," Tansy said quietly.

"Are you okay? Have you met up with Helene and Natasha yet? What is going on?" Cosmos fired quickly.

"Take a breath, Cosmos, so I can tell you," Tansy chuckled. "Yes, I'm okay," she replied, ignoring Mak's snort of disagreement. "Yes and no, we met up with Helene and Natasha yesterday, but they were called back to work. Seems the local Politsia doesn't like the fact me and the 'huge, ugly ass alien' you sent left behind a warehouse full of dead bodies. By the way, I need to talk to you about that. This is one of your bad ideas, Cosmos. I don't know what the fuck you created, but I don't think Earth is ready for it," Tansy said with reproof. "Anyway, we are on our way to meet up with Helene and Natasha. As for what is going on, it is bigger than I thought. You are in danger. I need for you to find someplace safe to hide until this is over. Avilov, the guy I was after, is involved in something big. Whatever information I stole has a lot of people pissed off right now. They have put a hit out for you and my family, not to mention, Helene and Natasha," Tansy said soberly.

"Don't worry about us. Natasha already called to warn me I might be in danger. I guess someone already tried to kill them. She and Helene are being careful. I've set up a bogus corporation and chartered a jet. RITA is taking care of spreading a ton of false trails that should keep them busy," Cosmos reassured her.

"What about Hannah? Is she with you?" Tansy asked as she nodded to let Mak know she saw the dark space in the rock face up ahead.

"Uh, no. She is safe though," Cosmos said hesitantly.

"What are you not telling me? I know my mom and dad went to this world you opened a door to. Mak told me," Tansy said impatiently.

"Oh. Well, Hannah and your parents went to help Tink," Cosmos replied in relief, thinking Tansy wouldn't mind.

"Are you telling me my whole family is on another planet?" Tansy asked through gritted teeth.

"Well, yeah. You have to admit they are safe there!" Cosmos responded with a positive tone.

"Cosmos," Tansy gritted out, clenching her fist around the strap of her backpack.

"Yes?" Cosmos' voice replied in uncertainty.

"You better be right. Once I get done untangling this mess, I am getting them back here and shutting whatever in the hell you made down. Just understand, if anything happens to them, I am not going to be happy with you. I have to go. Get your ass to a safe place until I can get there," Tansy muttered before hanging up.

CHAPTER THIRTEEN

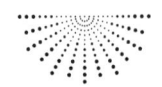

It was after nine that night before they entered the city limits of Ramenskoe. Mak slowed the old Volvo they had picked up in the cave to a crawl as they looked for the pub Helene had mentioned.

Neither one of them had talked much on the trip, lost in their own separate thoughts for once. Tansy spent almost as much time fighting the urge to connect with Mak as she did with trying to put the pieces of the puzzle together on what was going on. The fact that Craig Knapp was involved in something shady was a no-brainer.

She just wasn't sure the extent of the 'what' and 'why' of his involvement. She needed to look at the information she stole. There hadn't been time to decipher it before. Avilov had gotten the notion he wanted to take their relationship to the next level right in the middle of her stealing it.

"Who is Branson?" Mak asked suddenly breaking her concentration.

Tansy jerked as if she had been shot… again. She sat up straighter in her seat and scowled out the window. Branson was the last person she wanted to talk about with Mak. It was none of his damn business anyway.

"No one," Tansy replied shortly.

Mak didn't say anything for a few minutes. He slowed and pulled into the darkened parking lot of the pub. Only a small sign lit the night with the pub's name above it. Tansy stared at the sign, determined to not give in.

"Then, explain to me why you were still untouched until I claimed you as mine," Mak said, shutting off the engine before turning in his seat to look closely at Tansy's closed face.

Tansy turned her head and glared at Mak with a hostile expression. "I wasn't a virgin," she retorted defensively.

"You have not been with a man before," Mak said confidently. "You did not bleed as I was told you might, but I could still tell you were untouched. I could feel how tight you were and I know I caused you more pain than you would have had if you had already been claimed before."

When Tansy didn't say anything, Mak continued. "I talked with your sister Tink and J'kar. He explained what happens with human women who have not been with a man before," Mak said calmly.

"You did what?! I can't believe we are having this conversation!" Tansy growled out in a low voice. "You actually talked to my baby sister about sex?" Tansy asked in disbelief.

"Of course," Mak said with a small teasing smile. "She has many interesting ideas. She explained about oral sex. I found it very arousing. I will do it to you often," he continued, ignoring her open-mouthed stare.

Tansy gaped at Mak in disbelief before shaking her head as a hot blush burned her face. She covered her face with her hands and groaned. Her baby sister was giving sex education classes to aliens. She knew Tink was a lot like their mom, but she would have never thought she was just as bad.

"I can't believe you talked to my baby sister about sex, let alone oral sex," Tansy ground out hotly. "Why on Earth would you do that?"

"I needed to know how I could please you so you would not be afraid of me," Mak responded honestly.

Tansy's scowl turned even darker. "You were planning on having sex with me before you even came here?" she asked, stunned.

"Yes. I knew you were my bond mate the moment I saw your image. I came to your world so I could take you back with me," Mak explained.

Tansy let out the breath she was holding and slowly counted to ten. She stared straight ahead, trying to understand everything he was telling her. Raising a hand to rub at her aching temple, she fought the overwhelming fatigue that seemed to be a constant part of her life. She really needed a vacation. Somewhere with white sand, blue skies, even bluer water, and not another living soul around, including delicious, sex-talking alien hunks.

"Why will you not tell me, *je talli*? Is he the one who put the shadows in your eyes?" Mak asked gently as he ran the back of his fingers down along the curve of her cheek. "Tell me," he whispered.

Tansy jerked away, unbuckling her seat belt and turning to face him defiantly. "I loved him and I killed him. Are you satisfied?" she bit out bitterly.

Tansy turned and fumbled for the door handle. She pushed the door open and climbed out. The air was frigid and bit through the leather of her jacket. She was so damn tired of being cold. She wanted to go to a place that was never cold again.

She turned to pull her backpack off the floorboard. She vaguely heard the driver's door open and close. She straightened, only to find herself wrapped in Mak's powerful arms. For being so big, he sure could move fast and was unbelievably quiet. She thought briefly about struggling, but the warmth of his body was like the sun and she stepped into his embrace, seeking the soothing warmth.

"I do not believe you could kill the man you loved," Mak said gently. "I will not press you further, but know this… you will tell me soon about him."

Tansy buried her nose into his chest and breathed in his soothing scent. "Why?" she asked in a muffled voice before pulling back so she could look up into his face. It was too dark for her to see him clearly, but she needed to try. "Why is it so important to tell you?" she asked quietly.

"Because the shadows in your eyes have torn at my heart since the first moment I saw your image," Mak murmured, brushing his hand along Tansy's cheek before he cupped it gently with one hand. He ran his other hand down her back, pulling her closer into the shelter of his arms. "I want to take them from your eyes and replace them with the brightest stars in the universe," he whispered before he pressed a tender kiss to her lips.

∼

Five minutes later, Tansy found herself sitting in a dark corner of the pub pressed up close against Mak's huge body. The inside of the pub was filled with smoke, smelled of stale alcohol and sweat, and was so dimly lit, Tansy could barely see three feet in front of her. None of that seemed to bother Mak who leaned back against the wall drinking from a bottle of vodka.

"You know that stuff will eat a hole through your stomach," Tansy murmured.

"It is not as strong as what we have at home," Mak grinned.

Tansy frowned, watching as a group of men at a table not far from them shifted a little. Her hand wrapped tighter around the pistol she had drawn the moment they sat down. She felt Mak's hand as it closed around hers. Looking up, she saw the silver flames in his eyes ignite in warning.

"They will not harm you," he said, quietly setting the bottle of vodka down on the scarred surface of the table. "They would be dead before they had the chance."

"I don't...," her voice faded and she just nodded.

She was too damn tired to fight with him right now. If he wanted to take out the bad guys for a little while, she would let him. All she wanted to do was eat, get warm, and sleep for the next twenty years, and not necessarily in that order. Unfortunately, life got in the way so those plans would have to wait.

At least, the sleeping and eating part, she thought as she snuggled closer to Mak in an effort to get warm.

∼

Mak let out a sigh of contentment as he pulled Tansy's smaller figure closer to his. He let his eyes scan the bar, taking in every detail. It was small, consisting of less than a dozen tables.

Only three of the tables were currently occupied, not counting the one where they were sitting. Mak let his eyes linger a little longer on the three males sitting at the far table near the hallway that led to the bathroom. He did not like the way they kept turning their eyes on his mate. He continued to let his gaze move to the others. There were a total of ten men in the room and one woman.

The blonde-haired woman was sitting at the bar talking quietly to a man sitting next to her. There was another man sitting on the other side of her talking to the barkeeper. Two other men sat at a second table near the door and one older man, who appeared to be sleeping off too much alcohol, sat at the table closest to them.

"I need to visit the little girl's room. Keep an eye out for Natasha and Helene," Tansy murmured, rising up out of her seat. She looked down when Mak gripped her forearm lightly.

"Something does not feel right. Be careful," Mak responded, lightly rubbing his thumb back and forth over the soft leather of her jacket.

Tansy bent over and brushed a quick kiss across his lips. "I've been doing this long enough to know when things are not what they seem," she reminded him before moving away with a slight sway to her hips and a small smile curving her lips.

Mak tensed when she walked by the group of men near the hallway to the bathrooms. Except for one male shooting her an inviting smile, none of the men moved. He slowly relaxed back into his seat, watching and waiting.

He didn't have long to wait. Tansy hadn't been gone more than a minute when the blonde at the bar stood up and headed in the direction of the bathroom. It could have been a coincidence, but he doubted it. He felt the rage begin to build at the threat to his mate.

He was about to rise when a surge of frigid air burst into the room as the door opened. All eyes turned to the new figures coming inside. Mak's eyes swept to the entrance to see what new threat might have entered. His shoulders relaxed slightly when he saw the slight figure of Natasha and Helene's spiky blue-blonde hair.

Natasha touched Helene's arm and nodded to Mak. Both women walked toward him, scanning the room as they did. Helene's lip twisted into a small snarl at the three men sitting near the hallway. The movement was so slight and the room too dark for the human eye to catch, but Mak did not have any problems recognizing the fact Helene knew who the men were.

"Things are about to get nasty," Helene said coldly. "Where is Tansy?"

"She went to the cleansing room," Mak replied.

"Cleansing... you let her go to the bathroom alone?" Helene practically snarled at Mak before turning on her heel and heading in the direction Tansy had taken only moments ago.

"A female followed her," Mak said to Natasha. "I was about to make sure she was safe."

Natasha sat down in the chair next to Mak, making sure to keep her back to the wall. She calmly removed her gloves and tucked them into the pocket of her thick coat. She nodded to the barkeeper who nodded in return.

"Your female will handle the threat," Natasha replied in a calm, low voice. "The barkeeper is a friend as is the man who looks like he is sleeping. Do not kill them. You may kill any of the others, including the woman. If you are opposed to killing a female, Helene, Tansy, or I will take care of her."

Mak glanced sideways at Natasha before rising up out of his seat. "I have no problems killing a female who threatens to harm my mate or my people," Mak growled out, pulling one of his short swords out from under his coat.

∽

Natasha shivered as Mak's figure seemed to grow to a massive size. She stared in fear and fascination as his teeth began to elongate and his eyes lit with dark, silver flames. At that moment she was thankful she was on the same side as he was. She had no doubt in her mind that he would not hesitate for a second to kill her or anyone else that threatened Tansy.

The two men at the bar turned at the same time, guns drawn just as the two men at the table near the entrance rose. Natasha didn't wait. She opened fire with the precision of an assassin, killing the two men standing near the entrance.

Mak moved with incredible speed, slicing through the two men at the bar even as Natasha turned to fire at the three men who were seated near the hallway. The men flipped over the table and began returning fire. Natasha kicked the chair out of her way, crouching down behind the table as holes opened up in the wall around her. She quickly inserted another clip into her pistol before rolling over to where the man who had acted like he was sleeping fired at one of the men trying to escape down the hallway. He struck him in the upper thigh before taking a bullet to his shoulder.

"Sacha!" Natasha called out frantically as she watched her long-time friend fall backwards.

"Just a flesh wound. Get the other two!" Sacha yelled out from behind a table.

Natasha rose up to fire at the remaining two men, but it was unnecessary. Mak had already dispatched with the men and was wiping his bloody short sword clean on their coats. Natasha hurried over to Sacha to see how badly he was hurt.

"Find Tansy and Helene!" Natasha called out to Mak.

"You stupid old fool! You were only supposed to watch over them," Natasha mumbled to Sacha as she helped him out of his jacket.

Sacha drew in a painful breath. "How could I not participate in some of the fun? You have to let an old man have fun sometime," he grumbled.

"You and your idea of fun," Natasha snorted as she pressed a handkerchief against the torn flesh.

CHAPTER FOURTEEN

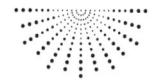

Tansy knew she was going to be followed. The woman at the bar had been a rookie. It would have been more believable if she hadn't been wearing a pair of Manolo Blahnik boots in a run-down little pub like this. She needed information and the pretty blonde was going to give it to her one way or another. Tansy was getting really tired of people chasing and shooting at her.

Tansy waited right inside the door. She leaned back against the wall and rolled her shoulders while she waited for the woman to enter. She almost rolled her eyes at how fast the woman followed.

Rookies, Tansy sighed. She hated killing them, but they only got better if you let them live. Unless this one convinced her differently, she wouldn't see another birthday.

Tansy reached out, grabbing the woman's arm that was pressed against the door as she pushed it open while wrapping her hand around the other one. She didn't wait to give the woman time to recover from her surprise. She pulled her around and shoved her face first into the wall hard enough to grimace when the blonde's face smacked the hard wall with a noticeable crunch.

Well, she could always have more cosmetic surgery if I let her live, Tansy thought in disgust.

Tansy pulled the woman's arm up behind her back at a painful level, forcing the knife in her hand to drop to the floor. Tansy used one leg to force the woman's legs apart, effectively immobilizing her.

"Who are you working for?" Tansy asked as she bent one of the blonde's fingers back. "Answer my questions the first time I ask and I won't break any bones. You don't answer or give me a bullshit answer and I'll start breaking every bone in your body one at a time."

The woman moaned softly but nodded her head up and down once to let Tansy know she would cooperate. "Avilov," she gasped. "Boris Avilov sent me."

"How many?" Tansy asked as she applied a little more pressure to the arm when the woman shifted slightly.

"The... the ones in the bar," the woman gasped before continuing. "Except for the barkeeper and the old man. There are three more outside."

"How did they know I was going to be here?" Tansy asked through gritted teeth.

"I don't know," the woman cried out as the pressure on her finger increased. "I swear! I don't know. I was just told to come here, capture you, and bring you back to him alive. If I don't, Avilov will kill me. He told us not to return unless we brought you with us."

Tansy worried about Natasha and Helene now. This is why she was better off alone. Then, she only had to focus on her own back. She personally didn't like to kill. She only took a life if she didn't have a choice or the person threatened the welfare of humanity. She didn't believe in playing God, but she did believe that some people were too evil to let live. Roberto San Juan and Boris Avilov were just two of those people.

"You have a choice...," Tansy started to say when gunfire erupted in the bar.

Tansy cursed when the woman threw her head back. She barely had time to jerk away. Even so, the woman's head connected enough of a blow to her chin she saw stars. Tansy reacted out of instinct, bending down low and kicking out a leg to try to sweep the woman's legs out from under her but her adversary proved to be a little more skilled than she anticipated.

Tansy felt the blow to her chest as one of those expensive Manolo Blahnik boots connected with her stomach, knocking her back into the sink. She twisted as the woman kicked out again, ducking under the outstretched leg and ramming her fist up into the woman's thigh, forcing her to back away.

"You stupid bitch," the woman said with an ugly smile as she jerked back and pulled out another knife. "You should have killed me when you had the chance."

"I may be stupid but you are the one with the broken nose, sweetheart," Tansy said, spreading her hands out in front of her. "I don't suppose you heard about the warehouse or the farmhouse for that matter or you wouldn't be feeling so confident right now," she added with a grin.

"Do you think I give a damn about them?" the woman scoffed as she moved closer to Tansy and took a swipe. "Avilov wants you back. He does not like it when someone steals from him. Where is the information you took?"

"Oh, it's in the hands of about a hundred people by now," Tansy goaded. "And not the politicians in Avilov's pocket."

"He is going to enjoy killing you slowly," the blonde smirked as she wiped her hand across her mouth, smearing blood from her broken nose. "I will enjoy watching."

Tansy shook her head sadly, looking at the blonde in front of her. "I really wish you hadn't said that," Tansy said softly. "I really do."

Tansy rushed the blonde, gripping the outstretched arm holding the knife and rolling her back into the blonde's body so she could push her up against the wall. At the same time they hit the wall, the door opened, knocking into both of them. Tansy twisted around, letting the momentum carry the knife still gripped tightly in the blonde's fist between them. The blonde's eyes opened wide as the knife embedded deeply into her stomach.

∼

"Tansy," Helene said breathlessly as she almost fell over her.

Tansy released the blonde whose eyes were already fading. She stepped back, letting the body fall to the dirty floor of the bathroom. She fought the bile that rose in her throat. It happened every time she took a life. It was only a matter of time before it was her body on the floor in some dirty, forgotten cesspool somewhere on Earth. She clenched her fists tightly and breathed through her mouth so she didn't have to smell the death mixed in with the urine.

"Come my friend, the men outside are dead," Helene said, gently touching Tansy's arm.

"When does it end?" Tansy whispered sadly before pulling away.

"Never, as long as mankind lives. There will always be those who prey among those weaker than they are and there will always be those of us who will stand up and fight to protect them. It is our blessing and our curse to care for things to be different," Helene said quietly as she wrapped her arm around Tansy's shoulders. "You have not recovered from your wounds. Come, we must leave."

Are you hurt? Mak's voice brushed across her mind.

No, Tansy answered soberly before erecting a wall to keep him out.

She wasn't hurt physically, but she felt like she had lost a little more of her soul tonight. She also accepted that this would be her last assignment. She knew deep down it would be.

Watching the blonde as her life faded away was almost like an omen. Tansy could almost see her own body being the one with the knife sticking out of it. She could not let her feelings for Mak go any further. It was time to make sure he returned to his world. She would close down the portal, then finish this once and for all.

Tansy shrugged off Helene's arm and gave her a stiff nod before she calmly pulled her pistol out and checked it. She opened the door to find Mak towering outside with a forbidding frown on his face. She pushed past him, ignoring his soft growl of displeasure.

"There are more men outside," Tansy said calmly, walking back into the blood-soaked bar. "If the blonde was telling the truth, there should be at least three more waiting for us. I am sure they have the exits covered and would have heard the gunfire."

Natasha looked up from where she was sitting next to the old man who had been sleeping at the table next to them earlier. He had a bloody bandage pressed against one shoulder. The barkeeper was sitting in the chair across from him, pouring him some vodka into a small glass.

"We will not have long once they realize we are not the ones dead," Natasha said, responding to Tansy's statement. "Cosmos secured a jet for us at the Bykovo airport. What do you suggest we do to get out of here without getting killed?"

"I'll go out first," Tansy said in a voice devoid of emotion. "They want me. I think it is time to give them what they want. I surrender, they take me to Avilov, and I kill him. I want you and Helene to take Mak back. You need to find Cosmos and have him send him home. It would be best if you both stay under the radar until this is over."

"No!" Mak ground out harshly, turning Tansy around to face him. "You will not give yourself to them. They plan to kill you."

Tansy pulled away and raised her gun, pointing it at him. "I know exactly what they plan. I told you before, I'm better off alone," Tansy said, moving backwards toward the entrance. "Don't think I won't shoot your huge ass. If it is the only way I can keep you alive, I'll do it."

Mak froze. "You do not have to do this," he said quietly. The flames in his dark, silver eyes burned with cold anger. "I can move faster than they can see, especially at night. I can see better at night, as well. I will find them and eliminate the threat. We will all go to the transport Cosmos sent together."

"No," Tansy said softly, shaking her head as she continued to back up. "This needs to end. My identity has been compromised. They know who I am. They will keep searching for me until they find me. In the meantime, they will use my family and friends as a weapon against me. I've sent the information I stole to multiple people, including my handler. It's time to end this. Go home, Mak. You should never have come in the first place," she said quietly before she turned toward the door and moved rapidly in an effort to get through it before she had to follow through with her threat to shoot him.

Mak sprinted after her the moment she turned, determined to stop her foolhardy plan. He refused to let anyone harm her. She did not understand either way would be death to both of them now.

He had claimed her as his. She bore his mark. She belonged to him and he would do anything to keep her safe.

He caught her just as she was about to pull the door to the bar open. Catching her arm as it swung around, he wrapped one hand around her wrist and applied pressure, while his other hand moved up to her exposed throat. He did not give her a chance to argue. He gripped her throat and applied pressure there as well. He saw her eyes widen in comprehension right before they rolled back in her head as she collapsed unconscious in his arms.

CHAPTER FIFTEEN

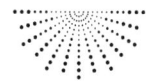

Tansy groaned silently as she slowly came to. Her head ached and her throat felt swollen and bruised. The constant fatigue still gripped her, but at least she wasn't cold. She struggled to make her foggy brain analyze the sounds around her. She could feel a strange vibration underneath her, she was lying down, her head was on a soft pillow and her feet were…

Tansy's eyes popped open at the same time as a curse burst from her lips. She was going to castrate a huge ass alien male! She was going to… All thought deserted her as said big ass alien male began massaging her foot in his big ass calloused hands. The curse turned into a moan of pure pleasure.

"I'm working really hard at being mad at you right now," she said huskily.

"I am working very hard right now at changing your mind about castrating me," Mak responded with a small smile as he continued massaging the arch of her left foot.

"You are doing a good job," she said honestly. Another soft moan escaped her as he applied just a touch more pressure. "So, do you often strangle the women you are with or was I just a special case?" she asked in a husky voice.

"You left me little choice. I could tell you meant it when you said you would shoot me," Mak chuckled. "I was not looking forward to that. It was much easier to render you unconscious until I could safely remove you."

She turned her head and looked at the luxurious interior of the jet. "What happened while I was out?" she asked.

Mak leaned back, picking up her other foot. "I went out the back door. The barkeeper turned off all the lights around the bar. Even with the item you call night vision goggles they were not able to keep up with me. I took out the three men who were waiting outside in a matter of minutes. Natasha and Helene borrowed a vehicle from the barkeeper's son, not trusting their transport might have been compromised. We drove to Bykovo where Cosmos had this transport ready," Mak explained as he worked his way up to her calf.

"How did they know where we were? The men who were there?" she asked as she felt her muscles turning to mush under his expert touch. "They were waiting for us."

"Helene's communication device was compromised," Mak said with a grimace. "She was very upset about it. That is why she had the old male called Sacha and the barkeeper there to help us until they arrived. They were detained when their vehicle exploded as they approached it outside their headquarters. Natasha was wounded and needed medical attention."

Tansy tried to sit up in concern, but Mak pushed her back. "How bad was it? Why in the hell didn't they just disappear? Where are they now?"

"We are here," Natasha said, coming from the front of the jet. "It was not that bad. I was more upset that Helene's car that she loved so much was destroyed. She had her favorite stuffed animal hanging from the mirror."

"You should have taken off and disappeared for a while," Tansy bit out with a worried frown.

"We have disappeared. Everyone thinks we are dead except for our family which we notified through a secured line. They knew this might occur. Cosmos set up extra security for my parents and brothers. We are used to living our lives like this since my mother and brothers were kidnapped," Natasha said, setting a tray of food down on a low table bolted to the floor. "You need to eat. We have a long trip ahead of us. We will be traveling to England, then France before making the journey across to the States."

Tansy reluctantly pulled her feet off of Mak's lap and sat up. She rubbed her hand over her throat and scowled at Mak before taking the offered cup of coffee from Natasha. She took a sip of the coffee before setting it down and turning to look at him.

"You were in my head again," she mumbled out. "I told you to stay out of it."

"I could no more stay out of your head than you can stay out of mine. Besides, the image of what you wanted to do to me before you opened your eyes was very vivid. It would have been difficult for me to ignore it," Mak said, picking up the plate Natasha had uncovered and placing it in Tansy's hands.

"What was she thinking?" Natasha asked curiously.

"Only that I was going to castrate him for knocking me out," Tansy mumbled again, but this time it was because her mouth was full of food. "You ever do that again and I won't just be thinking it," she added, pointing her fork at him.

Natasha stood up with a wince and chuckled. "I think I will leave you to each other. You are well suited. Both hot-headed and dangerous," Natasha added as she smiled down at Tansy, who was eating like it was the first meal she had eaten in a year. "I am glad he is on our side."

∽

The trip took almost seventy-two hours. Cosmos, or more than likely RITA, had smoothed the paper path for them. A complete packet of documents, including passports, money, and all government required identification were on board the jet when they arrived.

Tansy was now the arm-candy to Mak's elusive Ukrainian millionaire businessman. Natasha and Helene were his secretary and personal assistant, according to the documents. The deception was sealed by the time they reached Paris with a bogus corporation and history established.

Tansy had never thought before about all the money Cosmos had, as he never acted like it was a big deal. But for him to be able to do the things he did in such a short time showed he was more than just an absent-minded scientist. Cosmos had a full team of experts meet them at Charles de Gaulle airport in Paris where they were transferred to a Boeing 757 with a full staff. In addition, his most trusted security team was aboard. They included a wide variety of expertise. A tailor and team of seamstresses measured all of them before they even took off before disappearing until about two hours ago when they brought in the dress, as well as several suitcases full of other items.

She, Mak, Helene, and Natasha met with the security team made up of ex-CIA, marines, and mercenaries. They had hashed through several plans before deciding because of Mak's size, and the impossible task of making him blend in completely, they would use his size to play down Tansy. None of them said a word about the fact they couldn't understand a word he said, or his burning silver eyes, or anything else. Either they were used to the unusual or Cosmos had given them just enough information to distract them from the truth.

Tansy brushed a piece of imaginary lint from the emerald green silk dress she was wearing. She smoothed a strand of her dark red hair back under the blonde wig she was wearing and looked in the mirror one last time to make sure her lipstick looked right. She looked the part of being someone's arm candy with her full curves shown off by the low cut front. The rest of the dress hugged her figure, showing off the hour-glass shape.

Thank goodness for double-sided tape, she thought as she leaned forward a little to check her mascara.

They would be landing in another hour in Washington D. C. Cosmos had set up a room for them in one of the most exclusive hotels with Natasha and Helene. He wanted to make sure they were visible and invisible at the same time.

She had just finished adding a touch more mascara when the door opened behind her and Mak stepped into the bedroom. Tansy's breath caught in her throat as he quietly shut the door behind him and locked it. He looked astonishing in the perfectly fitted suit Cosmos had tailored for him.

Mak's eyes locked on Tansy. He released the fists he had clenched when he walked into the room and saw her. He gave up fighting the need to keep distance between them. He had been hard as a stone since he first saw her image and the feeling had only grown stronger the more time he spent with her.

He needed to feel her, hold her, and love her to help calm the storm building inside him at the thought of her being in the center of danger. They had little time to be alone since he found her and he was impatient to take her from this world so he could have her all to himself. He didn't care how selfish that made him seem. He had never cared what anyone else thought, well, except for maybe his parents, brothers, and sister.

"Mak," Tansy started to straighten from where she was bent over the dresser in the elegantly decorated room.

"No!" Mak's voice came out sharper than he expected. "No, stay like that," he said in a quieter voice.

Tansy watched his reflection in the mirror. His face looked strained as if he was having a difficult time controlling his emotions. Her eyes lifted to his and she stared, mesmerized by the heat burning deep inside. A shiver of desire coursed through her and she knew she was about to be well and truly taken. Her womb clenched at the thought and she could feel the dampness between her legs as her body responded to his.

"Mak, you shouldn't... I don't... you can't...," she tried to speak, tried to convey that this was a huge mistake.

"It is too late, *je talli*," Mak said quietly as he came up behind her. "It was too late the moment I first laid eyes on your image. I knew you were mine."

Tansy's eyes burned with unshed tears. *I can't face losing you too. I need to know you are safe somewhere out there.* Tansy didn't realize she had voiced her deepest fears.

We are one, je talli. Forever our souls are bound as one. It is the way of my people, our people. I can never leave you, Tansy, je talli, Mak's voice whispered across her mind.

~

Mak walked slowly toward her until he stood behind her. He refused to release her gaze as he watched her in the mirror. The sight caused a sharp shaft of pain to slide through him as need pulsed in his blood, calling for him to take her as the Prime warriors of old took their mates when they raided long ago.

He gripped her hips between his large hands, rubbing his hands over them through the fabric of her dress. He pulled her back until she was pressed against his swollen cock. He wanted her to know his need, his desire. The women of his world would have shrunk in fear at a male's strong desire, but not this tiny human female. She met him head-on, fearless with her own need.

The women of his world seldom, in his experience, enjoyed the act of copulation, but not this delicate human female. She took from him and gave even more in return. It was believed over time the Prime male evolved to produce the chemical needed to arouse the female. But one look from this delectable human female and he was about to go up in flames without ever having to sink his teeth into her.

Mak had wanted to talk to her privately before they landed. He knew she believed she could send him back to his world alone. He knew she planned on going after the men who were chasing her alone. He also knew he would never let that happen.

All thoughts about arguing with her, bullying her if necessary, flew out of his mind when he walked in and saw how beautiful she looked. He wanted to rip the blonde wig she was wearing off her head so her beautiful red hair would flow down her back the way it had when they had come together before. He yearned to wrap her dark red strands in his hands while he took her over and over.

His eyes slid down her figure where the dress clung to her body. The look in her eyes when she first saw him sent waves of molten desire through his veins. She could deny it all she wanted to, but she felt as deeply for him as he did for her.

His need for her surged to a painful level when he heard her breathing become erratic and a soft moan escaped her sweet lips. He had to touch her, take her, and claim her as his own before they landed. He had not said the words binding them together as bond mates, but he would now. Nothing would ever separate them.

He slowly released her hips so he could undo the button and zipper on his pants, pushing them down until his straining cock was freed. Pushing gently against her back, he forced her to lean forward over the front of the dresser. He gripped the silky material of her dress, gathering the material in his hands before pulling it up over her hips.

Mak ran his calloused fingers along the smooth, soft skin of her ass until they stopped on the sides of the lacy undergarment she called panties. His eyes rose so he could look deeply into her dark green ones. He smiled wickedly at her.

"I hope you are not attached to this material. It is not going to be usable again," Mak said as he snapped the sides between his fingers. They both groaned when Tansy pushed back against him as the material fell away.

"Oh God," Tansy whimpered. "I want you so badly I hurt," she moaned out impatiently.

Mak chuckled at the need in her voice. "I expected you to resist me," Mak said as he slid his fingers down to stroke her.

His breath released in a loud hiss as his fingers encountered the swollen, slick folds of her cunt. "Tansy, I need you now," he growled out, aligning his pulsing cock with her swollen vaginal channel.

"I claim you as my bond mate. My wife. For always, *je talli*," Mak said hoarsely as he pushed deeper inside her. "Gods and Goddesses, Tansy," Mak practically howled as he felt her grip his cock. "I have never felt this way before!"

"You damn well better not have," Tansy growled back as she leaned forward and gripped the edges of the dresser. Her head fell forward as he pulled almost all the way out and pushed back in, driving deeper. "I'm not going to last long this way," she added breathlessly as he hit every nerve ending both going in and coming out.

Mak grabbed her hips and began rocking faster and harder. He would claim her again and again. He wouldn't be able to stop himself from doing so. The joy of having his bond mate burned through his soul. He needed to repeat his claim of her in his own language and would release the mating chemical into her again. Suddenly, one hour did not seem like such a very long time as heated moans filled the cabin of the huge jet.

CHAPTER SIXTEEN

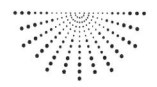

Tansy shivered as the cool evening air brushed against her exposed shoulders as they walked out of the entrance of the airport. She had changed out of her emerald silk dress into a black and white halter top with matching wide-legged trousers. It had a matching jacket, but she forgot it when she finally stumbled off the plane.

Correction, she thought as Mak pulled her closer to his side, *I had to find something else to wear after Mak shredded the emerald green dress I had been wearing. And my legs are so damn shaky from all the different ways he took me. Girl, you are in some serious trouble!* Tansy muttered silently.

They had landed without incident almost an hour ago. The processing through customs went faster than Tansy expected. She had anticipated some type of delay, but it appeared RITA was an expert at creating forged documents and uploading all the necessary information to the right computers. She could almost hear RITA's sigh of exasperation at Tansy having any doubts about her ability. Hell, as far as Tansy knew, the government didn't even have a computer as smart as RITA yet.

Tansy glanced at the man walking beside her. Mak's huge shape dwarfed the men sent as his bodyguards. She would have laughed if the situation hadn't been so tense. Cosmos had sent a cryptic message to her new cell phone. She had tried to reach him on the satellite phone, but he didn't reply. Now she knew why.

Gone on an exotic vacation with a friend. Aunt Rita says 'hello'. The door is open, but you will need the key. It is in the mailbox at your parents place. Don't forget to pay your quarterly taxes. Your accountant says it is past due and you are in deep trouble. The head of the firm is looking for you. Tell your boyfriend, his friends will be looking for him soon. Love you, Cosmos.

Cosmos had gone through the gateway presumably to get help. He left information with RITA on how to get through the gateway and where to find what Mak would need to get back home. He also warned her that she was in deep shit.

It looked like this went all the way to the top and her handler was warning her to proceed with caution. To top all of that off, she was now going to have to deal with the fact there were going to be more aliens running around. She was ready to ship them all back to their own world, get her family back, close the damn gateway, and clean house. Then, she was going to go find herself a deserted island somewhere and play castaway for the next few years.

My brother, Borj, has an island not far from his home near our ocean. I will take you there, Mak said. *But, know this, if the gateway is ever closed, I will be on the same side of it as you are.*

Tansy groaned silently in annoyance. *Can't you just stay out of my mind? I have enough going on inside it without you butting in all the time. Do you have any idea how you screw up my thinking when you talk to me this way?*

I will never be able to keep from touching your mind. And I enjoy screwing you, Mak whispered, unconcerned that she was irritated with him. *Over and over and over, again and again.*

Will you just stop it already? God, you must have been taking lessons from my parents! I thought once a man did 'it' that they couldn't do it again for a while? How is it possible for you to have done it three times? And in less than an hour? Tansy muttered crossly.

I am not human, Mak said, glancing down at Tansy's flushed face.

Tansy rolled her eyes. *Like I haven't figured that part out. I can't wait to send your huge ass back home;* she muttered, ignoring the sharp pain in her chest at the thought of never seeing him again.

You are a very stubborn female. Has anyone ever told you that? Mak asked, frowning down at her again before moving to one side so she could get into the limo parked at the curb waiting for them.

Has anyone ever told you that you are very annoying? Tansy asked impatiently as she slid quickly in.

No. At least, no one who has lived afterwards, Mak said seriously.

Tansy rolled her eyes, again. She wasn't even going to ask what he meant by that comment. She sighed in gratitude when Natasha leaned into the limo and handed Tansy the jacket to her pantsuit. Tansy pulled the jacket on with a grateful smile and leaned back against the seat. She chuckled when she heard Mak's sigh of relief when he slid in behind her. He was happy at not having to fold himself up into a ball in an effort to fit into the car.

Helene had laughed when she told Tansy earlier about their trip to the Bykovo Airport. They had come close to tying Mak's big ass on the roof of the barkeeper's son's car. He had not been happy about their joking and even unhappier after the trip from Ramenskoe to Bykovo.

He was stretched across the seat as far as he could go and was still folded almost in half. To top that off, he had to sit with her unconscious body draped across him the entire way. He said that was the only reason he survived it. Helene and Natasha both thought that was hilarious.

"Knapp will be searching for any unusual arrivals," Tansy said as the limo pulled away from the curb. "He would have made sure all incoming flights from overseas were reviewed carefully. We won't have much time before he tracks the plane we arrived on."

"By the time he realizes we are here, we will be gone," Mak said quietly as he stretched his long legs out in front of him. "If he is stupid enough to come for you, I will kill him."

"We go with the plan we set up," Tansy said coolly, looking at Rico, the head of their security team. "Rico, do you have the equipment I requested ready for me?"

There were only five people in the limo, Tansy, Mak, and Rico in the back, and the driver and another security guard in the front. The rest of the team, including Helene and Natasha, followed in several unmarked SUV's. They would meet at the hotel at different times over the next couple of hours.

A dark smile crossed Rico's face, pulling the scar near his mouth. "Of course," he replied in amusement. "When this is over, the two of you should think about doing one of those reality shows. The spy and the…," he paused a moment, returning the intense silver glare Mak was giving him. "I don't know what in the hell you are, man. Cosmos… he has helped all of us one way or another over the years so we don't ask him too many questions about what he does; but, damn if you are from any place I've heard of."

Mak grinned, letting his canines lower just a little. He chuckled when Rico let out a curse, scooted further away from him, and made the sign of the cross. Tansy rolled her eyes, let out a snort, and back-handed him in the chest.

"Knock it off," she hissed. "No scaring the locals. You know you are supposed to be acting like you are human."

"I don't even want to know what that means," Rico muttered under his breath in Spanish.

"Don't worry, I'll be sending his big ass home shortly," Tansy said before she turned to look out the window as they passed the Capitol building.

∽

Tansy closed her eyes and breathed deeply. They had checked into the hotel room several hours ago. The rest of the team was scattered along three floors, one upper, one lower, and the same as her and Mak's suite of rooms.

They would move out tomorrow night. Tansy had RITA download the information she stole to a new laptop Cosmos had sent with the rest of the gear Tansy had requested. She also had RITA break into Knapp's email and check his schedule. He was expected to be at a charity function tomorrow night with several other key members of the defense department. Right now, she needed to take a closer look at the information that men on two continents were more than eager to kill her to get back.

She sat down and powered up the computer. Rolling her shoulders, she entered her password and waited as the files opened. She paled as she began reading it. No wonder Boris was so determined to get this back. He had signed his own death warrant by even having half the names on the files. Tansy began opening each one, reading, memorizing, and swearing. If the information was correct, then this did go almost all the way to the top. It stopped at the second-in-command. This was going to blow the lid off the government as she knew it.

"Fuck!" she whispered as her mind reeled at the depth of deception.

"What is it?" Mak's deep voice asked as he walked out of one of the bedrooms in their suite.

Tansy looked up and stared at Mak for just a moment before she stood up and walked over to the window overlooking Washington, D. C. Her mind was in turmoil. She had to make a decision. It didn't seem to matter which scenario she chose, none of it looked good for her. The bad guys wanted her dead, and after what she was about to reveal, even the good guys would think it better if she was no longer around. It was a lose-lose situation, at least for her.

"There is a charity event tomorrow night that I need to attend," Tansy began in a slightly husky voice. "You won't be able to go with me," she turned to look at him and held up her hand before he could argue with her. "You are too visible and different. It would cause more problems and endanger more lives. You can stay with Rico and back me up if I need help."

Mak's lips flattened into a straight line of disapproval. "Let others take care of this matter," he said harshly. "I will not let you go alone."

Tansy looked carefully at Mak before she turned back to stare out the window again. "I have to go alone. I have to be the one to finish this," she said softly.

"Why?" Mak bit out harshly walking up to stand behind her. "Why must it be you? There are others who can do this."

Tansy's gaze focused on the figure standing behind her before she became lost in the dark memories that sucked at her soul. She wrapped her arms around her defensively as she let them out of the box she kept them tightly concealed in. A cold shiver ran down her spine, seeping into her bones until she felt like one of the many statues that adorned the city.

"My parents are two of the most exceptional people I've ever known," she began quietly. A small smile curved her lips as she thought of them. "They are supportive, smart, talented, creative, and very much in love," she added with a hollow chuckle. "I don't think there is much that isn't positive about them. Most of all, they are very giving," Tansy took a deep breath before continuing. "When I was fourteen my mom was asked to go to South America to look over some type of equipment for an oil company. All of us were excited. We enjoyed the traveling, but the idea of not living in a motor home for a couple of weeks was really exciting to three girls sharing a closet size bathroom with their parents."

Tansy turned to look at Mak before she crossed over to a chair and sat down on legs suddenly weak. The fatigue continued to drain her both mentally and physically. If she survived this, it was a good thing she planned on it being her last assignment. Right now, she felt weak as a kitten.

"The first days were wonderful. We were staying at the head of the oil company's compound. Each of us had our own bedroom and bathroom. It was heaven," her voice trailed away as she stared out the window, not seeing the glittering lights of the city but the dark shadows of her memories.

"Until...?" Mak prompted gently as he moved to sit across from her on the couch.

Tansy looked at him, blinking several times to bring the vision of him and not what happened back to her mind. "Until the night a group of men attacked. There was a dinner followed by dancing afterwards. Hannah got to stay up an hour later because she was the oldest. Tink and I were supposed to be in bed, but I was too excited. I snuck back down the stairs and hid under one of the tables," she murmured. "It was so grand and everyone was having so much fun. Hannah was dancing with a really cute boy that had been following her around all evening when suddenly a group of armed, masked men burst in. They began firing randomly around the room. I saw the security guards grab my parents and the other two couples from the oil company and take them out of the room. The boy dancing with Hannah was shot..." Tansy's voice faded for a moment as if she suddenly had trouble getting the sound to come out.

She jerked when she felt Mak slowly entwine his own larger hand with hers and squeeze it gently in encouragement. She tried to pull back, but he refused to let her go. Truthfully, she didn't want him to. She slowly relaxed enough so she could continue telling him why she was who she was.

"What happened next?" he asked.

"They took her. They took Hannah," Tansy said, clearing her throat. "There was nothing I could do. I was trapped under the table by two of the people who had been shot. I heard the death rattle in their chests as they died. I couldn't get out. They took her," she whispered in a broken voice.

Mak cursed silently at the tears in Tansy's eyes that came to the surface but refused to fall. He knew deep down that this was just the beginning of her story. He wanted to go back to when she was so young and wipe away what happened to her. This was one of the reasons Prime males were so protective of their females. While there had been war and conflicts, it was the male's responsibility to protect the females from having to witness such atrocities.

"Yet, she is with my brother," Mak said gently. "She was found?"

She shook her head slightly. "Yes and no. She escaped from the camp where they were holding the group into the jungle. She survived for ten days before she came upon a small village along the river. A couple cared for her and contacted my family," she explained quietly. "Hannah... Hannah was never the same, though. For a long time she would have horrible nightmares. She refused to talk about what happened to her during the time she was held. Even now she refuses to say anything about it. She also can't stand being around a lot of people. There are very few people that she trusts," Tansy's lips twisted into a smile that never reached her eyes. "I can understand why."

"Who was Branson?" Mak asked, suddenly understanding that was where her story was leading to. This male was the one who put the dark shadows in her eyes.

"Branson," Tansy said softly, looking again out the window without seeing anything. "He was my teacher, my friend, my lover if you could call him that, and the only person I've ever really trusted besides my family and Cosmos. He taught me everything I know. After seeing what happened, what those men did, and what they took from my sister, I knew I could never let that happen to anyone else. I could never let *them* do that to anyone else. So, when I was eighteen I left my parents and started searching for someone who could teach me how to stop people like the ones who took her. I began hanging outside of bars, listening, asking questions, learning."

The deep growl that escaped Mak's chest was evidence of his displeasure at the idea of her being exposed to so much danger. Tansy chuckled and shook her head. "Branson felt the same way. He came out of one of the lesser quality establishments I had chosen one night to find me surrounded by four men. It didn't take long for him to send them running with their tails between their legs."

"What did he do next?" Mak asked with a frown.

Tansy looked at Mak with a sad grin. "He grabbed my arm, jerked me down into his lap, and gave me holy hell for the next half hour before letting me go. Here was a man in a wheelchair and he was able to defeat four huge ass biker dudes. I knew he was the one to teach me what I wanted to know," she said.

"He should have refused," Mak growled out, not in the least liking this 'Branson' at all.

"He did... for the next three months. I camped out on his doorstep, dogged his every shadow, and begged him until he finally gave in. I told him if he didn't teach me I would go back to the bars and find someone who would," she said, pushing a strand of dark red hair back away from her face and letting her head drop to rest against the back of the chair. "For the next year, he pushed me. At times, I didn't think I would survive, but every time I thought of giving up, he asked what would have happened if Hannah had given up when she was alone in the jungle with those men. Who would have helped her? How could I not be at least as strong as she was to not give up? He knew how to play the guilt card and get results," she muttered softly before continuing. "Branson was older than I was by almost fifteen years. He was an ex-Special Ops. He had moved into a special program the government started. He was caught during his last assignment and tortured. They broke his back, paralyzing him from the waist down. He was forced into early retirement. He later joined a group of men from his unit who had formed a security company," her voice broke again as she talked about the man who had changed her life. "He was the smartest, kindest man I ever knew. The only thing he wanted to do was make the world a better place to live, a safer place. He had grown up on the streets. His parents divorced and he never knew his dad. The gangs were his family until he went into the military. It was there he found his niche in life."

Mak watched as silent tears slid down Tansy's pale cheeks. He hated seeing the dark shadows under her eyes and the even darker ones in them. He could feel the deep sorrow and pain inside her as if it was his own. The darkness of loss was eating away at her.

"What happened to him?" he asked in a somber tone.

Tansy's tear-filled eyes turned to look into his. "Me," she whispered. "Me," she repeated with a small sob.

He couldn't stand the pain anymore. Reaching out, he pulled her resistant body into his arms and held her tightly, refusing to let her go. He rocked her small, fragile form as silent sobs shook her. There was nothing he could do but give her some of his strength as she struggled to finish her story.

"I refused to give up going after the men who had hurt Hannah. I wanted them to pay for what they had done to her. She was no longer the laughing, happy girl anymore. She was so quiet afterwards. She would stare out the window for hours and I could hear her crying at night. They took a part of her away that I wanted back. I wanted my big sister back and they took her away!" she said bitterly. "Branson told me revenge was not the answer. That it could never bring Hannah back to who she was before. He told me that in order to prevent something like this from happening to someone else's sister that it was necessary to take out the man or men who order the killings and abductions in the first place. He said it was important to take out the leaders to break the chain of command," she mumbled against his chest. "So, I found out who it was and I went after them."

Mak's arms tightened protectively around her smaller form. The vision of what she was about to share exploded in his mind. "They struck first," he said hoarsely.

"Yes," she replied dully. "They struck first. Somehow, there was a leak warning them that someone was going to come after them. They were told it was Branson. I had gone to meet my parents and Tink for dinner. Branson was working on another assignment and decided to stay home. They came for him," Tansy couldn't say anything else out loud.

She doesn't have to, Mak thought in despair as the images of what she found formed in his mind in vivid, colorful detail.

Tansy had returned to find Branson strung upside down from the beams in their living room. He had been tortured and gutted. His remains had been scattered around the house as a warning.

A message warning that anyone who decided to come after them would suffer the same fate was written in Branson's blood on the wall of their living room. Even their pet cat had not escaped the brutality of the attack. Its head was placed in the refrigerator and not found until several days later when Tansy was cleaning out the weapons cache Branson had hidden.

"I killed them," Tansy murmured in an emotionless voice. "I killed them all. I went after each one of Roberto's men who was involved and killed them. I wanted him to know someone was coming for him next."

Mak didn't say a word. He just held Tansy tight. He could feel her fear that she was nothing but a cold-hearted murderer. She believed she was no different than the men she had killed, but he knew better. He saw the images of her rocking the young girl who had been brutally molested and beaten. He saw her helping the families of the men who were murdered for rescuing the hostages who were taken with her sister. He saw dozens and dozens of ways she helped to direct the young boys and girls who had taken the wrong path and joined gangs find a different type of family, away from the violence of the streets. But, there was still something she was holding back from him. Something very important had happened since they had checked into the hotel. There was a resolve in her that had not been there before.

"Why is it so important for you to do this and not someone else," Mak asked quietly.

Tansy pulled back enough to stare up into his eyes. "I know who really betrayed Branson now. I never knew who had. I knew who did the actual killing, but I never could figure out who was the one who had betrayed him, until now," Tansy said with a hard edge to her tone. "I know who it is and I'm going to kill the son-of-a-bitch if it is the last thing I ever do."

Mak held Tansy's small body tightly against his own. She had woken several times during the night. He was so tuned to her mind now, that each nightmare became his own. The first time he woke her by making love to her hard and fast. The next few times he simply pushed his own thoughts into her dreams, taking over through force to change them to his own. He could feel the exhaustion still pulling at her. Her mind refused to slow down or stop long enough to let her get the good, deep rest that she needed.

He needed to find a way back home. He was afraid for the first time in his life… afraid he would not be able to keep his mate safe. She was determined to kill the man responsible for her ex-lover's death.

He had been right when he said she had not been with a male before. It was true, she hadn't been a virgin as his brother J'kar described, but she had still been untouched. Her relationship with Branson could only go so far due to the physical limitations forced by his injuries.

Regardless, he could feel the deep love and sadness she had for the other man. A part of him was surprised at the lack of jealousy he felt at her feelings for another male. Perhaps it was because the man was dead, but he was more inclined to believe it was because he was thankful for the guidance and protection the man had given to his mate when she was younger. If he had not taken her under his wing, she might have not met with someone who could teach her how to have survived until he came into her life.

The sun was beginning to rise when he felt her stirring again. He knew the exact moment she woke fully. He felt the heat of her anger. Mak rolled over, caging her between his arms and under his body.

"You were doing it again," she glared sleepily up at him.

He brushed a kiss over her lips and grinned down at her. "Who... me? Would I ever sneak into your mind without your permission?" he asked, trying to look innocent and failing miserably.

Tansy's lips twitched at his teasing. "Since I didn't say anything about you being in my mind... yes, you would." Her eyes softened for a moment before she continued. "Thank you."

Mak groaned at the bashful look in her eyes before he buried his head into her shoulder. "You never have to thank me for being there for you. I love you, *je talli*," he whispered. "It is my right to care for you."

Tansy released a small embarrassed laugh and hugged him close for a minute before her stomach let out a loud growl. "Well, I hope that care includes a shower and food. I could really use both," she sighed out.

Pulling back until he was looking back down at her, he grinned again. "Yes, except for one problem. I would use your communication device to order food for you, but the person on the other end would not be able to understand me," he said with remorse.

"I've got that covered," a voice from the door said.

Tansy's head jerked around at the unexpected intrusion and she uttered a loud curse. "Damn it, Cosmos! You scared the shit out of me! What are you doing here?" Tansy asked, shocked.

"I was worried about you, but I should have known the big-ass alien male I sent to you would have you covered," he said with a grin from the doorway looking at Tansy peeking out from under Mak's huge, partially covered figure. "I just wasn't expecting it to be quite so literal," he joked while raising his eyebrows up and down.

Mak growled out under his breath. "I should have killed your ass when I had the chance before," he snarled out playfully.

"Why would you want to kill Cosmos?" Tansy asked, puzzled, looking up at Mak then over at the door where Cosmos shifted uncomfortably.

"I'll go order some food," Cosmos quickly said before disappearing into the other room.

Mak chuckled and looked down between his and Tansy's body at her full breasts pressed against his chest. "He made a comment about your breasts."

Tansy looked up at Mak, shocked for a moment before she pushed against his chest, trying to get him off her. "God, what is it about men and their fascination with a woman's boobs?" she asked, rolling out of the bed. "It must be a genetic thing pre-programmed into every male, regardless of what planet they come from."

"Why should we not be fascinated with something so beautiful?" Mak asked, enjoying the view of Tansy's ass peeking out from where her hair hung down her back as she walked to the bathroom.

Turning, she flashed her eyes suggestively at him. "Well, if you are that damn fascinated, why don't you come show me?" she asked with a mischievous smile before disappearing into the bathroom.

Mak let out a curse under his breath as his cock swelled in response. He would have to be dead not to hear the invitation in his mate's voice. He practically fell out of the bed trying to get untangled from the sheets wrapped around him.

In all his existence, females had been afraid of him. Gods, even the males feared him! How he was blessed to find a bond mate who was not only unafraid of him, but met him head on in every way was beyond his comprehension. The fact that this tiny human mate was not intimidated by his size humbled him. He couldn't wait to introduce her to his mother and sister. They were the only other females who were not intimidated by his size.

A dark frown crossed his face as he thought about his sister. Where was she if Cosmos was here? Who was protecting her? A low snarl of rage burst from his lips. His gaze swung from the bathroom door where he could hear his mate bathing to the door leading into the other room. He groaned and ran his hands through his hair in aggravation. Grabbing his pants, he shoved his legs into them before he strode to the door, pulling it open so fast it banged against the wall. Cosmos was hanging up the phone when Mak reached for the front of his shirt.

"Where is Terra and why are you here?" Mak growled out, annoyed.

"Hey!" Cosmos said, startled as Mak continued pushing him until he was up against the wall near the door leading into the hotel room. "She's safe! I swear I wouldn't have left her if I didn't think she was safe," Cosmos choked out.

"Mak! Let him go!" Tansy said from the doorway of the bedroom.

Mak's eyes darkened when he saw his mate standing there with nothing more than a towel wrapped around her lush figure. Her hair was hanging down like wet ropes of flame and her dark green eyes sparkled with fury. He was about to tell her to go back to their room when a whistle of appreciation whipped his head to the other side. He let out a deep growl of warning as he stared at the other three men in the room. He had been so focused on Cosmos and finding out about Terra that he neglected to see if there was anyone else in the room.

Tansy shook her head at the other men and moved forward to try to save Cosmos who was beginning to look a little blue. "Let him go, you overgrown ox! No killing the good guys and definitely no killing my baby sister's best friend!" Tansy growled back, gripping the towel in one hand while smacking Mak in the arm with the other.

"Go get dressed," Mak snarled quietly under his breath. "I do not want the others to see you unclothed."

"I'll drop this towel and let everyone and their brother see me if you don't release Cosmos this instant!" Tansy snarled back.

"I have no objections to you holding him a little longer," one of the men said hopefully.

"Me either!" the other said with an appreciative grin on his face as he stared at Tansy's long legs. "For someone so small, the female has long legs and is..." He broke off when Mak dropped Cosmos and turned on him.

"She is mine!" Mak snarled out, moving into a defensive stance between her and the other men.

"I think we figured that out from the scent on her," the last male said drily. "Besides, we have learned to be careful around human females. They can be very painful if you get too close and they don't want you to."

Mak turned with a soft expletive and watched as Tansy helped Cosmos to his feet, barely keeping her towel on. He pulled her against his body, ignoring the glares she was giving him. Tansy looked over at the three huge males standing and sitting near the small dining table in the room.

Each had dark silver eyes, but only one had short hair. The other two wore their hair a little longer than Mak did. She tilted her head and studied them as closely as they were studying her. None of them were as tall or as broad as Mak was. He towered over even these men who made her feel like an ant in an elephant's pen.

"Let me guess, you are Mak's friends," Tansy said dryly.

One of the men came forward only to stop when a growl escaped Mak. Brock, his brother's head of engineering, stopped a few steps away. Merrick, Leader of the Eastern Clan, and Lan, the palace's head of security, watched from where they were sitting on the couch and chair.

"Go get dressed," Mak hissed out under his breath. "In fact, stay in the bedroom until I get rid of them."

"No way, Tarzan," Tansy said drily. "My name is Tansy, not doormat. I'll get dressed, but I'll be right back out here. Cosmos, did you order some food? I'm starving."

"Yea… yeah!" Cosmos said, rubbing his throat with a scowl. "Dude, you have got to quit trying to choke me," Cosmos said with a glare at Mak. "I just got healed from the last time."

"Where is Terra?" Mak growled out, swinging around to look at Cosmos while trying to keep his eye on Tansy.

"She's with Tilly and Angus. Tilly promised to keep her hidden from everyone but your mom," Cosmos said gruffly. "Do you think I would be stupid enough to leave her here when there might be a threat to her?" Cosmos bit back sarcastically. "I told you I would kill anyone who tried to take her from me."

Tansy's surprised gasp drew all eyes to her again. "You… kill someone? Mr. Laid-back-never-get-stressed-out?"

Cosmos raised his middle finger at Tansy with a grunt. "Screw you, Tansy. I might be a scientist, but I know how to do more than you think."

Tansy chuckled. "I'd love to see that! By the way, thank you for all your help getting me out," she added softly, walking up to him and brushing her lips along his chin. "I thought for sure my time was up."

Mak released his breath in a deep sigh before bending and picking Tansy up, making sure the towel caught under his arm so her ass wasn't showing. He ignored her squeal of indignation and outrage. If she wouldn't leave the room on her own two feet, he would pick her up and take her.

"You are mine!" he bit out. "That means no showing your body to other males, no kissing other males, and listening to me when I tell you to do something."

"In your dreams, King Kong!" Tansy snorted out, ignoring the astonished looks and chuckles as he slammed the door to the bedroom behind them.

～

Forty minutes later, Tansy leaned back with a happy groan and rubbed her full belly. She almost snorted when all conversation stopped and five pairs of men's eyes followed her movements. She guessed it could have something to do with the silk, white dress she was wearing.

The designer had done an excellent job of tailoring it to emphasize her curves. The neckline was modest but still showed a substantial amount of cleavage. She had left her hair down and it fell in glossy waves of rich, dark red to her waist. She had added a touch of makeup to bring out her eyes and high cheekbones. She knew she looked good, but it still amazed her when guys acted like they had never seen a good looking gal before.

Not good-looking, beautiful, Mak whispered with a flash of desire in his eyes.

Whatever, Tansy whispered back in exasperation.

A knock on the door interrupted their conversation. Tansy glanced in warning for the men to be quiet. They hadn't heard from Rico or the others this morning. It was possible it was them at the door. Tansy picked up the small pistol she had set down on the table. Rising, she moved to answer the door when the knock sounded again.

"Wait," Mak growled out, nodding to the other men to spread out just in case.

Tansy paused long enough for the men to move into several different spots. She waited for Mak to give her the sign to continue. Pushing a strand of hair back, she stepped to one side of the door.

"Who is it?" she called out in a light cheerful voice.

"Rico and company," came the cheerful, slightly accented response.

Tansy unlocked the door, recognizing their code that all was safe. "Hey Rico, morning, Helene, Natasha," Tansy said as she turned and walked back to the table and her coffee. "Have you guys eaten yet? Cosmos ordered plenty and there is still some coffee left."

"Thanks Tansy," Rico said, heading for the cart filled with food. He stopped and paled as the other men came out from where they were hidden about the room. "Madre de Dios, Cosmos! There are more?!" Rico swore as he glanced warily at Lan, Brock, and Merrick.

Cosmos grinned at his old friend before slapping him on the shoulder. "Hey Rico. What's up?"

"I'll tell you what is up, my friend... my blood pressure. You seemed to have forgotten to tell me a few things about this assignment," he muttered as he walked cautiously over to the cart and poured himself a cup of coffee.

Brock and Lan started when they heard the feminine chuckles following Rico's muttered comment. "You should have been there when Natasha and I first saw Tansy's man. He scared the shit out of me," Helene said as she started to walk over to the cart as well.

She had only taken a few steps when Brock stepped in front of her with a low rumble escaping. She jerked back, startled, and glanced up at him in surprise. She must not have been happy with what she saw in his eyes because she turned with a sharp glare to Cosmos.

"Call off your hound dog or I'll put a leash on him," she snapped out, trying to walk around him only to find herself stopped again when he stepped back in front of her. "VChat te futsk?" she cursed in Russian.

Brock glared down at Helene. "What did she say?" he demanded, frowning.

"She isn't happy you are blocking her way to the food," Natasha laughed as she walked over to the couch and dropped her jacket on the end of it. She winced as she straightened and held onto her side. "But, that is...," Her voice died as she found herself trapped suddenly.

A low growl sounded from the man standing in front of her. "Tansy?" Natasha called out quietly, a slight quiver in her voice was the only indication she was unsure of the man towering over her.

Tansy was having a hard time keeping from laughing. Helene was looking at Brock with no small amount of hostility. Natasha, on the other hand, was standing like a deer caught in the headlights of a semi, looking at Lan with raised eyebrows. Her hand had moved to the pistol tucked in the back of her waistband. Both of the men were emitting a low, rumbling growl.

"Mak, call off your friends before Helene and Natasha shoot their asses," Tansy said, sipping her coffee while Cosmos looked on in exasperation, Rico looked on in horror, and Merrick looked on with resignation and a slight amount of envy.

Mak said something sharply to the two men and they glared at him for a moment before taking a reluctant step back, giving both women more room to move. Helene and Natasha looked at the men warily before edging around them and moving to the same side of the table as Tansy.

"Cosmos, you need to tell your new friends to not mess with your old ones," Helene bit out as she filled a plate with food. "We don't necessarily fight fair."

"Natasha, are you okay?" Cosmos asked in concern when he saw the brief flash of pain cross her face as she leaned over the cart and lifted the carafe of coffee.

Natasha waved her hand nonchalantly. "I'm fine, just a little stiff and sore still," she replied, pouring herself a cup of coffee and moving back to the couch. "The stitches are pulling and some of the bruises are being a little difficult. Nothing that a few more days will not cure," she added with a stiff smile.

"You are hurt?" Lan growled out menacingly, taking a step toward her again.

Helene snorted. "She is lucky she is not dead! If she had been a foot closer when my car exploded, we would not have been able to pick the pieces of her out of what was left of it," Helene said grouchily.

"I am just glad both of us were not injured any more than we were," Natasha said, settling back into the cushions. "Tansy, Helene and I will accompany you to the charity function tonight. I will go as a guest..." Natasha began.

"And I get to go as the serving girl," Helene mumbled glumly. "Why do I always have to be the serving girl?" she grumbled.

"Because you are the one who insists on having blue hair," Natasha said with a smirk.

Helene's eyes flashed in mock outrage. "I can be a rock singer!"

"Yes, but what if they ask you to sing something? No one would believe it then," Cosmos said, reaching over Helene's shoulder to grab a piece of bacon.

A grunt escaped him when Helene elbowed him sharply in the stomach. "I was drunk when you heard me singing," she said, glaring at him. "That does not count."

"That wasn't the only thing you were doing," Cosmos whispered in her ear before he jerked away from her elbow again.

"You can't prove anything," Helene snapped back with a grin. "I destroyed all the video surveillance from the club that night."

Cosmos was about to say something else, but Brock took a menacing step toward him. Cosmos decided he had enough bruises around his neck from Mak and didn't want any more. He looked carefully back and forth between Brock and Lan. If looks meant anything, the way Brock was glaring at Helene, and Lan was hovering around Natasha meant the two women were about to find themselves in the same boat he was in.

Cosmos looked down at the intricate circles on his left hand before he clenched it tightly into a fist. He had a feeling there was going to be a lot of missing persons reports filed soon. Sometimes he really wished he hadn't invented that damn gateway. No sooner had that thought formed in his mind, so did another. Only this one was of a slender, dark-haired alien beauty with burning eyes of silver.

Shit, he thought in aggravation, he was in serious trouble.

CHAPTER SEVENTEEN

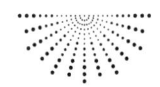

*T*ansy smiled demurely as she accepted a glass of champagne. She let her eyes sweep the elegantly dressed patrons attending the charity function at the Canadian Ambassador's house. RITA had created the invitations she and Natasha were using and added them to the list of guests. She was going to have to take a closer look at the programming her mom was doing. She never really appreciated just what a genius her mom was when it came to inventing things until now.

Cosmos either, she thought as her mind instinctively reached out for Mak.

I am here if you need me, je talli, Mak's soft words flowed through her mind.

I know, I know, Tansy responded, making sure she didn't roll her eyes in exasperation.

It had taken her most of the afternoon to convince him to let her go. She had never met such a stubborn, hard-headed, arrogant…

Wonderful mate, he said, finishing off her thought.

Whatever, she sighed as she took a sip of the bubbly drink in her hand.

I will be here if you need me, he repeated before she felt him pull back until he was just a shadow in her mind.

Tansy's eyes paused on Natasha, who was charming the ambassador from Norway before she let them continue their sweep. No one would have noticed the slight tightening of her hand around her glass. It was the only outward sign she gave that she had finally found her target… Craig Knapp, Senior Director for the Collaborative Partnership against Terrorism, or CPAT as the group Tansy belonged to was called. He was talking to the wife of the German Ambassador and a well-known singer from a popular country group.

She smiled at the waiter as she set her glass down on the tray and walked over to where they were talking. She knew Craig wouldn't recognize her right away in the get-up she was wearing. She had dark brown hair piled into an elegant French twist with decorative silver beads threaded through it. She wore more makeup and brown contact lenses. Her dress was an exclusive Zuhair Murad Paris design.

The gold evening gown had a deep vee going all the way down to her belly button and no back except for the delicate gold chains draping down the slender curve of her spine. The wide semi-sheer sleeves allowed her to hide some well-placed accessories. Her feet were encased in delicate, four-inch gold strappy heels.

"Buonasera," Tansy greeted the small group in a husky Italian. "The ambassador outdid himself as usual, sì?"

"Yes, he and his wife always do such a wonderful job and for such an important cause," the German ambassador's wife agreed.

Tansy smiled charmingly and turned to the singer, complimenting her on her recent Country Music Award. The next ten minutes were given to relaxing the small group. Tansy gave Craig undivided attention whenever he said anything, leaning into him, and giving all the signs she was hanging onto his every word.

The looks he was giving her in return showed her he was more than happy to have that attention. When she would turn slightly to one of the women, she noted the flash of irritation that crossed his face briefly. She knew she had him when he moved in closer to her and placed his hand on the small of her back. She leaned back into his hand to let him know she was aware of him.

Move away from him, now, the deep voice of one angry alien male echoed loudly through her mind.

Tansy smiled at the ambassador's wife as she fought the desire to roll her eyes at the demand. She turned her head just enough to catch a glimpse of Helene's smiling face. The chic glasses she was wearing had a camera embedded in them. Mak was watching everything she was doing from the command center they had set up in a plumbing van a block over.

Her eyes moved to Natasha who was charming the Director of CPAT. From all of the information Tansy had gathered to date, Brad Taylor appeared to be on the up-and-up. Nothing showed he was aware of what his Under Director was doing.

Her eyes moved to several other men who worked in CPAT. Three of them were involved and would be falling with their boss. Two of the other men were low-end operators, programmers, paper-pushers, nothing to worry about from what RITA had gathered.

"Yes, I would love to get a breath of fresh air," Tansy said with the slight accent she had perfected during the three months she spent in Italy during one of her assignments two years before. "It has been a pleasure talking with you," she bowed her head graciously to the other two women who continued to talk about the possible upcoming tour the singer was doing in Germany.

"You are breathtaking," Craig murmured close to Tansy's ear as he let his hand dip from the skin on her back to the swell of her ass.

Tansy forced her body to remain relaxed even as he squeezed his hand. She dipped her head down to keep the look in them from being seen. She glanced up just in time to see Helene looking at her with a raised eyebrow. Helene adjusted the glasses and glanced to where Craig's hand was before she moved her gaze back up to Tansy's face with a smirk.

The loud growl that exploded through her head caused her to flinch. Tansy smiled apologetically. She leaned into Craig, forcing her body not to shudder. Everything in her screamed for her to pull away from him. She had never felt such an overwhelming need to get away from another human being before.

Tansy, you have to move away from him, Mak's voice said coldly in her mind. *I will not be able to tolerate another male putting his hands on you. This was not part of the plan.*

Actually, it was. It was just the part of the plan I kind-of forgot on purpose to tell you about, Tansy replied.

Tansy shivered as Mak's cold rage flowed through her. She would never be able to carry this through convincingly if he kept growling, snarling, and threatening her. There was only one thing she could do and she knew he was going to be royally pissed at her… she had to completely shut him out like he did to her back on the farm in Russia.

Tansy smiled seductively at Craig as he drew her closer to his body. She rubbed against him slightly as he asked the attendant for her fur coat. She gave a breathless giggle as he brushed a kiss along her neck as he draped her coat over her shoulders.

"Tonight you are all mine, my gorgeous little beauty," Craig murmured in her ear.

Tansy turned her dark brown eyes to his, a small, tantalizing smile curving her plump, red lips. "Oh, yes," she breathed out.

∾

Mak burst out of the van with a snarl. He was going to wring his mate's scrawny little neck. He never should have let her go. He should have known it was too easy. Her agreeing to have Natasha and Helene nearby should have been his first clue she was up to something.

Her agreement to let them monitor what was going on from a van a block away was the second. Her agreeing to let anyone else be involved was a glaring third. How he could have forgotten her insistence that she worked alone he would never know, or make the mistake of ever forgetting again.

He glanced wildly around, trying to determine which way to go. He had been in the back of the van with Rico and two other men so it took a moment for him to orient himself. He reached out to Tansy again, only to encounter a wall higher than the mountains on his home world of Baade. He snarled, turning in a circle. Frustrated, he reached for the communication device Cosmos gave him.

"Merrick, Lan, Brock, my mate has gone off with the human bastard," Mak snarled out fiercely. "Do you have her in sight?"

Cosmos' voice came over the link. "She's getting into a limo with Knapp. I'll track her. Damn it, Mak! I thought you talked to her!" Cosmos bit out furiously sounding slightly out of breath.

"I did! That does not mean she listens to me," Mak snapped back. "Where are you?"

"I'm coming along the sidewalk on the south side," Cosmos said hurriedly.

"Shit!" Rico's voice exploded over their ear pieces.

"What is it now?" Mak said as he ran down the alley and turned the corner, almost running into Cosmos as he broke into a run.

"Natasha and Helene are in trouble! I just caught a glimpse of a guy grabbing Helene and shoving her out through the kitchens. Another has Natasha," Rico cursed under his breath. "We've been made. Fall back and regroup! Mike, get us the fuck out of here!"

Mak heard the sounds of soft thumps of metal being hit followed by the sounds of wheels squealing from the direction he had just come. He turned to go back, but was knocked sideways by Cosmos who tackled him just as several small bits of concrete from the wall burst where his head had been.

Mak rolled, pushing Cosmos off of him. His eyes narrowed on the direction the firing had come from. In a swift move, he drew one of his sharp small knives and threw it as hard as he could. A gasp, followed by a gurgling sound came from the direction.

Mak rolled to his feet, ignoring Cosmos, and strode rapidly over to the frozen figure. A man dressed in a suit and overcoat stood impaled against the wall. Mak cursed when he saw he had struck the man through the heart. The knife went through him into the brick building. He grabbed the handle and yanked it free, wiping the blood on the man's coat as he fell.

"Where is my mate?" Mak snarled softly to Cosmos as he came up behind him.

"I have RITA tracking her," Cosmos said, paling as he looked down at the bloody body. "Rico has met up with Team One. Team Two is tracking Natasha and Helene. Lan and Brock are with them. Merrick was chasing down another guy who was coming up on us from the west," Cosmos said, pulling out a small device.

"The limo isn't heading for Knapp's place. It looks like it is heading toward the Navy Yard. I have a couple of my guys on their tail. We are headed your way and will meet up with you on the other side of Capital Street. Move your asses," Rico barked out.

"Let's get the hell out of here," Cosmos said.

"I am going to kill that bastard and anyone who is with him if he harms one hair on my mate," Mak said coldly.

"I'll cover your back while you do it," Cosmos said quietly, breaking into a fast jog.

CHAPTER EIGHTEEN

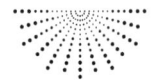

Tansy realized the moment she stepped into the limo she was in trouble. She recognized the scarred face of the man sitting across from where she was pushed none too gently. She turned her head just enough to shield the dismay in her eyes before he saw it.

She had met up with the son-of-a-bitch twice before. Once when she first joined CPAT and another time when she came across him on assignment. He had gone off the deep end, killing almost a dozen innocents. He had been terminated from the program and had supposedly been killed while on a mercenary assignment in the Philippines.

"How's it going, Tansy? Beautiful as ever," Drew grinned wickedly. "I have to say, though, I like the red hair and green eyes better than the brown on brown."

Tansy didn't even bother with playing games with the man sitting across from her. "I have to admit I like you better dead instead of alive. By the way, how was the Philippines?" Tansy asked, crossing her legs. "From the way your face looks, I'd say it must have been a blast," she added with a nasty grin.

She enjoyed the flash of anger that crossed his face. He always did like being a pretty boy and there was no way anyone would ever call him that again. The right side of his face was puckered and ridges of scar-tissue crisscrossed it from his brow to his chin. The look in his blue eyes promised she would regret that little pun.

"You think this looks good, wait until I get done with you," Drew said with a tight smile pulling his mouth to one side. "I'll make sure you live a little longer than your boyfriend did. What was his name... oh yeah, Branson. Now I remember. I wish you could have heard him screaming as I ran my knife through him. Oh yeah," he gave an ugly laugh. "You couldn't hear him because I cut his tongue out."

Tansy felt like her blood was freezing as she listened to Drew talk. "You're a worthless piece of shit. I'm going to enjoy killing you," she hissed out, jerking toward him with her hands curled into claws.

Craig grabbed her arm in a bruising hold and jerked her back into her seat. "You don't know how much it disappointed me when Drew told me who you were. I never would have seen through your little dress up, but he did almost immediately. What gave her away, Drew?" Craig asked as he lit a cigarette and inhaled deeply before releasing it with a deep sigh. "It really doesn't matter, of course, but I'm curious. I still plan on enjoying your beauty before I let Drew have his fun."

Tansy jerked away from Craig's touch, settling back into her seat. "Yes, Scarface, what gave me away?"

Drew's eyes narrowed, but he ignored her little dig. "No one has a body like you do, Tansy. Those big, plump breasts, tiny waist, perfect rounded ass made for fucking, and lips created just to make a man come between them," Drew said with a dark, hot gaze.

Tansy reached up and carefully undid the dark brown wig she was wearing, palming the tiny, silver balls and clips in her hand. She plucked the pins out of her own rich red hair and let it cascade down her back. Shaking her head, she let the heavy length hide the fact she was pocketing her stash in a small slit in her gown.

She smiled coolly at Drew. "You forgot to mention my hair. Men love my hair," she breathed out in a husky voice known to cause a man to harden just from the sound. "And you, Two-face, will never know what it is like to have my lips wrapped around you," she finished coldly.

"You fucking bitch," Drew said, raising his hand to backhand her.

"Stop!" Craig's sharp tone sounded loud in the quiet of the limo. "You can have her after I am done with her. I don't care what you do to her then, but I want her before you start marking her up."

Tansy's eyes narrowed into a deadly glare at Craig Knapp. "You know I'll kill you before you can do anything? What is in it for you? Why would you betray your country?" she asked coolly.

Craig drew in a deep drag of his cigarette and blew a smoke ring at Tansy. She fought back a cough and waved her hand to dissipate the smell. Drew chuckled at her obvious distaste.

"I am loyal only to myself," Craig said with a smile. "Money can give a man more comfort than being a patriot, isn't that right, Drew?"

"Damn right," Drew answered, relaxing back as the limo turned down a side street toward a length of old warehouses along the Potomac River.

Tansy looked out the darkened windows and grimaced. She was really beginning to hate warehouses. These didn't look any better than the ones in Moscow.

It wasn't quite as cold outside, but it was still colder than what she was looking forward to. She tried to bring a picture of a nice warm beach with silky white sand under her as she lay in the sun, enjoying a cool drink while she soaked up some rays. She closed her eyes for a moment and wished her life had been a little different. She was right back to where she started just weeks ago.

She released a tired sigh as the limo slowed down. It inched through an opened gate that was quickly closed after the limo passed through. She knew this was going to be her last assignment. She had fought for closure ever since Hannah was kidnapped over ten years before.

She had wanted justice for Branson's death. Now, it looked like it was all coming together. She would have closure and peace at last.

And don't forget you wanted to know what it was like to truly love someone one more time, a small voice in her head murmured.

She had found all of it. The only thing she wouldn't be able to do is say goodbye to her family in person. She hoped they knew how much she loved them.

She was sure they would once RITA gave the message she left for Cosmos to give to them. She had left one for Mak, too. Regret filled her that she had never told him out loud that she loved him. She knew she couldn't leave this world without telling him how much their short time together had meant to her.

Tansy turned her head to look at Craig Knapp, who was sitting so arrogantly next to her. "Why did you order Branson's death?" she asked, suddenly needing to know the truth. "Why? He was no longer working on any projects for CPAT."

Craig looked intently into her eyes before he snuffed out his cigarette butt in the glass of whiskey he had poured earlier. "He was getting too nosy. He was working as a consultant for a company working for CPAT in the same region of Africa that he had been in when he was hurt. When his team pulled him out of the Congo I knew it was only a matter of time before he made a connection to the ties I had there. The nice thing about being almost the boss is no one really pays much attention to you, but you know what everyone else is doing. Avilov, San Juan, and I had a very lucrative business going. The U.S. backed the money to the rebels, Avilov supplied everything from drugs, to girls, to guns, and San Juan transported it all where it needed to go. All I had to do was make sure nothing interrupted the flow of things, like the U.S. getting suspicious when the items they were supporting didn't end up where they thought it was going to," Craig nodded to Drew. "Drew here was my main man. He eliminated anyone who got too close. Branson was sniffing around and had discovered information that should have been destroyed... from you. You got him curious about San Juan which is where he followed the link to me. I have to admit I was surprised by you. You were just some naïve little girl set on revenge. I never expected you to survive Branson's training, much less a year in the field. When you took out San Juan, I was more than a little curious about you. That is why CPAT drafted you into their program. It made it easier to keep an eye on you."

Drew grinned as the limo came to a stop inside a warehouse along the edge of the river. "I was a little put out when I showed up to kill San Juan only to find him dead. His men were scrambling to find out what happened. That was slick, making it look like a heart attack. The only thing I could get out of the guard I had to kill instead was that San Juan had a beautiful red-haired señorita with him. No one knew what happened to her. All I found was that little bitch dead in his bed," Drew chuckled out.

Tansy exploded at his nonchalant attitude of the death of a little girl. She reacted in fury. Kicking her leg out, she let the spiked heel of one of her delicate, but deadly sandals pierce the neck of the man sitting across from her. She ground her heel in, twisting it.

Craig pulled a handgun out and pressed it against Tansy's temple. "Let him go," he said calmly, ignoring Drew's gasping as he struggled to breathe.

Tansy dug the sharp point of one heel into his neck a little deeper while the other one cut into his groin. "Her name was Sonya," she hissed out coldly, not moving either one of her heels until she had made her point.

Craig pushed on the barrel again to remind Tansy he was there… like she needed a reminder. She slowly released Drew, watching as he grabbed the hole in his neck, trying to stem the flow of blood. Only when she was seated back against the soft leather of her seat did Craig lower the gun.

"You bitch," Drew snapped out hoarsely. "I am going to skin you alive and enjoy listening to you screaming while I do it."

"Hey, Drew," Tansy said with a smile, flipping up her middle finger at him at the same time. "The lab called, your brain was too rotten to save so they want me to put you out of your misery."

Drew pulled a knife out of his pocket and flicked it open. His eyes narrowed dangerously as he glared at her. He started to lean forward, but stopped when Craig turned the gun on him instead.

"I told you, after I am done with her," he repeated in a calm, cool voice.

Drew closed the knife and put it back in his pocket. He pulled out a handkerchief and applied pressure to the wound on his neck. The dark promise in his eyes sent a shiver down Tansy's spine. Against her will, she reached out to Mak, needing to feel his warmth one more time.

I am here, je talli, Mak responded in relief to her touch.

I just wanted to tell you I love you, Tansy whispered as she thumbed one of the silver balls and hair pin in the palm of her hand. *I wish things could have been different. Goodbye.*

CHAPTER NINETEEN

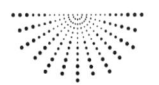

Mak turned and gripped Cosmos by the shirt, pulling him to a stop. He could tell from the fear and resignation in his mate's voice that she did not have much time. He had to get to her and he had to get to her now.

"Do you have the portable gateway with you?" Mak asked grimly.

"Yes, but you know you can't use it to get to her from here to there. It is too dangerous," Cosmos said, drawing in a deep breath.

"True, but I can use it from your world to mine and back again. Do you have the coordinates to Tansy?" Mak insisted.

"Yes," Cosmos said excitedly as he realized where Mak was going. "But, if you go to her this way, you'll be alone."

Mak's lips curved into a dangerous, deadly smile. "Then, I won't have to worry about killing the wrong people," he said in a tone that sent a shiver of dread through Cosmos.

"Take this," Cosmos said, thrusting the portal device and the GPS tracker he had for Tansy. "RITA can program it in while you get what you need."

Mak nodded, taking both devices. He slid the GPS into the pocket of the jacket he was wearing. "Find the others. Tell them to stay clear of where they have taken Tansy. I will kill anyone who is near her."

Cosmos nodded. "Mak...," Cosmos said, reaching out and placing his hand on Mak's thick forearm. "Bring her home safe."

Mak gave a sharp nod and turned the dials on the portal. He watched as the gateway shimmered. Without another word, he strode through it into the portal control room on Baade. Within seconds, the portal had closed behind him.

Cosmos stared at the darkened space for a moment before he opened communications with Rico and Team One. They had two other women to rescue and three aliens to send back home before anyone discovered them.

It was going to be a long night, he thought as he picked up speed to intercept the van.

~

Mak burst through the portal into the control room in the palace. Derik was talking with their father, Teriff. The look on Mak's face was enough to let both his younger brother and his father know that something bad had happened. He ignored both of them as he brushed passed them.

"Mak, what is it?" Teriff asked, jogging up behind him. "Is there danger to our world?"

"No, my mate has been taken by human males who wish to kill her. I must go to her," Mak snarled out, slamming through the door to his living quarters.

He shrugged out of the leather jacket he was wearing, grabbing the GPS unit out of it first before throwing it against the wall. Walking over to a clear panel, he muttered a phrase and watched as it slid back. Inside, he had a cache of weapons. He quickly began pulling items off the shelves.

He snarled out when he felt his father grip his arm in a hold that stopped him. Few men on any world were strong enough to hold him. His father was one of those few. He looked at Teriff with a look of defiance, daring him silently to try to stop him.

"I will come with you," Teriff said with a grim smile. "It has been a long time since I have had a good fight. I like my new daughter's family very much. I have seen the pain that human males can inflict. Your brother Borj almost lost his mate to one. I will not lose you or my other daughter," Teriff said gruffly.

Mak stood frozen for a split second before he gave a jerky nod of appreciation. "I would be honored to have you fight by my side," Mak said as he slid a harness over his head and adjusted it across his massive chest.

The harness was quickly filled with a wide variety of weapons. He would not take a chance with his mate's life. His only focus was to find her and get her to safety. He didn't care how many men he had to kill to do it. He quickly slid two short swords into their sheaths on his back.

Teriff ripped his shirt off and reached for an assortment of weapons of his own. He gripped a couple of laser pistols before sliding them into the holsters on his hips. Reaching for a long double-sided blade, he couldn't keep the grin from his face even as he prepared for battle.

"Did I tell you that I did almost this same exact thing when I kidnapped your mother from her village so many years ago? It took a while for her family to accept me because of that. They wanted her to mate with a male from her clan, but I knew she was mine the moment I saw her," Teriff said as he adjusted the sword.

Mak turned, looking at his father with his mouth hanging open. "You kidnapped mother?" he asked sharply.

Teriff grinned at his son for a moment before he turned to grab a handful of small explosives. "Yes, I was hunting when I came upon her village and decided to take her. Remind me to tell you about it when we get back," Teriff said as he turned around to head out the door. "Tilly says it was love at first sight. Did you know she captured her mate as well? She said something about tying one on and having her wicked way with him. I had never heard of such a thing before."

Mak shook his head and grabbed a Med kit from the shelf before he gave the command for the panel to close and followed his father out the door. It would seem there was a great deal he did not know about his own family. He only hoped he and his mate survived long enough to learn more.

Mak and Teriff pushed back through the door of the control room.

Both of them stopped and frowned at Derik, who stood next to the doorway holding up three portable devices. That was not what stopped them. What did that was Derik. He was dressed in full battle gear.

"What are you waiting for?" he asked defiantly.

"You are staying here!" Both men growled out at the same time.

"No! I have just as much right to help as you," Derik said, looking at his father in anger. "I am a Prime warrior," Derik growled out in a low voice.

Teriff looked at his youngest son. It was true. By the time he was Derik's age, he had already been to battle several times. There was no way he could deny his youngest son's desire to protect the human females. He was very attached to them, especially the one called Tink.

"You stay focused and listen to your brother and me. If you get hurt, your mother will be angry with me. I… do… not… want… her… angry! Do you understand?" Teriff growled back, pointing his thick finger into Derik's chest.

Derik grinned. "What are we waiting for? RITA, do you know where Mak's mate is?" Derik called out.

"Already programmed the devices, sweetheart. I'm putting you as close as I think it is safe based on the satellite images I have in my databases. Don't worry about your mom. I'll keep her occupied so she doesn't know you are gone. Bring Tansy home safe," RITA said even as she opened the gateway door.

∽

Tansy's skin felt chilled even in the heated interior of the limo. She focused on slowing down her breathing. She palmed several of the small silver balls in her hand. She had five of them. She had appropriated them from the front of Mak's vest without him knowing earlier in the day and hooked them into her hair band.

She had been more than a little impressed with the holes they left back at the farm outside of Moscow and figured they might come in handy. If she couldn't shoot or stab the sons-of-bitches, she would blow them up. Even if it meant blowing herself up with them. At least the world would be down a handful of assholes. She could only hope the information she had sent to several of the other agents, her handler, and the Director of CPAT was enough to encourage them to go after Avilov.

Tansy turned her head when the limo driver opened the door for Craig to slide out. She hated it when he motioned for her to slide out next. She didn't like the thought of Drew being at her back. Trying to minimize the amount of time her back would be turned, she slid across the seat while pushing one of the small pins into the ball. She hoped the information she got from RITA was accurate, otherwise she was about to become a bloody blob on the concrete floor.

She hissed when she felt Drew's hand slide down her ass and between her legs as she reached for the door to help her stand up. She dropped the silver ball into the door grip and moved away from the limo as far as the driver and Craig would let her go.

She counted down in her head as she did. She had maybe forty-five seconds to get away from the car before it exploded. When she was down to twenty, she swung around, catching Craig in the chest with her knee and pushing him into the driver.

"You bitch!" Craig gasped out as he fell against the man standing next to him.

Tansy didn't wait to see what happened next. She sprinted for one of the beams supporting the roof of the warehouse. She heard Drew cussing as he struggled to get out of the car. Several other men yelled out as she ran and she heard the sound of gunfire. Since she didn't feel any striking her, she had to assume Craig still wanted her alive.

She reached out, grabbing the cold steel beam just as the car exploded in a thunderous roar that echoed throughout the building. Palming another explosive, she didn't bother with setting a timer to it. She threw it in the direction of the men.

As soon as she released it, she kicked off her sandals and took off running, ignoring the frigid concrete beneath her feet. She had to get out of there before she was trapped. She knew Craig would not bother waiting to kill her any longer. The explosion shook the building with such force it knocked her off her feet, throwing her a good three feet before she fell.

Tansy rolled as she hit the hard floor. She looked over her shoulder trying to determine who was where. She could see what was left of the limo lying upside down and burning. The driver was dead, his body twisted in an unnatural angle.

She shuddered when she saw Craig roll the body off of his own. He was bleeding in multiple places from what little she could see. His right arm lay limply against his body as he rolled over and slowly got to his feet. His right pant leg was torn and bloody as well.

Tansy glanced frantically around, looking for Drew. She didn't see him anywhere. He had either not gotten clear of the limo before it exploded or had been thrown away from it.

All she knew was she had to find cover before they recovered. Rolling over, she stumbled to her feet. There was a set of stairs leading to the upper floor.

If nothing else, she could find a place to hold them off. She had three explosive devices, a small nine shot pistol, and one knife. She would just have to make sure every shot and explosion counted. She was almost to the stairwell when she felt the burning heat of the bullet as it struck her in the arm. She cried out as it cut through her.

Forcing herself forward, she fell onto the metal steps, ignoring the way the sharp edges cut into the side of her thigh as she hit it. She pulled the small pistol from under her left arm, which was hanging useless beside her, blood pouring from the agonizing wound.

"You're dead, Tansy!" Craig called out hoarsely. "There is no escaping. I have twenty men here. No one can help you."

"Fuck you, Craig," Tansy yelled back. "And I think you need to work on your math. You might have had twenty men, but not anymore," Tansy responded, moving up a step at a time while keeping her eyes open for anyone coming at her from either above or below.

"Doesn't matter," Craig responded, wiping the back of his hand across his face and smearing blood from the numerous cuts on it. "I shot you. You won't last long with being wounded."

Tansy laughed bitterly. "Like you think I haven't been shot before? I escaped Avilov and I was shot worse than this!"

Tansy was over half way up the steps now. She refused to think about how cold she was beginning to feel or how tired. She was always tired and cold.

A small movement out of the corner of her eye had her rolling over to the wall. She fired, relying on experience and intuition. Both served her well when the body of one of Craig's men fell over the railing above her to land with a sickening thump on the floor below.

"Another one down," Tansy muttered through her clenched teeth. "God only knows how many more," she wearily added under her breath.

She only hoped that if she were going to die tonight, it would be swift. She had no intentions of letting Craig or any of his men get hold of her.

Tansy scooted up several more steps. She was almost to the top. There was a thick beam at the top of the stairs and an open door off the end. Pulling out another one of the explosives, she gathered her strength. She would throw it and haul ass up the stairs into the room. She could only hope there was no one else up there.

"You might as well give up, Tansy," Craig said, moving closer. "If you do, I might just kill you quickly."

"Did anyone ever tell you, you would make a lousy politician?" Tansy called out. "How about I do the world a favor and just kill your ass. I tell you what. I won't even make false promises! I'll do it quickly," she added just as she tossed another precious explosive over the railing.

Tansy pulled herself up and with a burst of adrenaline she ran up the remaining steps, throwing herself through the doorway just as another explosion rocked the warehouse. Tears poured down her cheeks as she landed on her bad arm. It was necessary so she could slide on her back with her gun aimed at any possible targets. The room was blissfully clear.

Unfortunately, she didn't have time to enjoy the brief rest her body was screaming for her to take. She rolled over onto her knees, cursing the nausea that was threatening to overtake her. She breathed rapidly through her nose and fought to focus. She reached out for Mak, desperate for just a brief touch of his warmth and strength. When all she encountered was a black void it nearly suffocated her in the emptiness she felt all the way to her soul.

Had something happened to him? Had he given up on her? What if he was hurt? Fear unlike anything she had ever known threatened to break the last fragile hold she had on her emotions. A soft sob caught in her throat as she reached out over and over for him only to encounter the same emptiness.

Pushing up to move further into the shadows, she found herself in a small room with no windows. There was only the one door leading into it. The echo of hushed voices coming up the stairs drew her attention as she moved as far back into the room as she could go. There was nothing to hide behind, nothing to squeeze through. Her luck had run out.

Tansy let her body slide down to the floor, leaving a bloody trail on the wall behind her. She pulled her legs up to her chest in an effort to counteract the tremors shaking her slender form. She reached for the last two explosives, laid her gun on the floor beside her, and waited as the voices came closer.

CHAPTER TWENTY

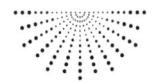

Mak moved through the gateway that opened into the still, frigid darkness outside a group of warehouses near a river. They were in an alley between two buildings. A high fence separated the buildings between them and another set that ran down to the waterfront. RITA had explained she was opening the portal far enough away they would not be seen, but close enough for them to get to Tansy's GPS position.

Mak felt his father touch his arm briefly before he nodded his head toward a dark figure standing across the road at the entrance to the fence. The man was staring intently through the fence at something closer to the water. They watched as the man stamped his feet before the bright glow of a flame lit the night briefly. A moment later the scent of an acidic smoke drifted to them.

Teriff motioned with his hand he would take care of the man. Mak nodded. Derik moved up silently behind him. He pointed to the back of the alley and made a circling motion with his hand. He would go around and take care of any threats that way. Mak nodded, looking up. He would go up and over the fence.

Each man focused on what they needed to do. Mak jumped up silently and gripped a metal bar attached to the side of the building.

Once he was sure it could hold his weight, he moved stealthily up the side of the building until he reached a small ledge.

Perching on it, he could see the area surrounding the warehouses. He scanned the region for threats. There were four men moving cautiously around the perimeter of the warehouse closest to the water.

Each had a weapon in their hand and from the looks of it, they were waiting for something. Mak pulled the GPS tracking device out of the pocket in his pants and looked at it. Tansy's signal was coming from the same place.

Sliding it back into his pocket, he watched as his father moved in along the building. At first he wasn't sure what his father was doing. He appeared to be walking as if he had drunk too much. His father stayed in the shadows, but made just enough noise that the man at the fence took notice. His father's voice, muttering in a low tone reached him. A grim smile curved his lips as he realized his father was using a distraction method to pull the man away from his post.

The man at the fence called out to Teriff who ignored him and staggered back until he slid down along the side of the fence still in the shadows. It looked like he was a drunk who had passed out.

The man at the fence muttered a curse and tossed his smoking stick to the ground, crushing it under his foot. Mak turned his gaze to the other four men. None of them were paying attention to what was going on by the fence. They were too intent on whatever was happening in the building.

Mak jumped down on the other side of the fence, landing silently on the balls of his feet, one hand barely touched the concrete before it moved to grasp one of the knives sheathed across his chest. He sprinted along the edge of the warehouse, keeping to the shadows as much as he could.

Behind him, he heard a soft gasp followed by silence and knew his father had dispatched with the man at the gate. The knowledge of years of training was the only indication Mak had that his father was joining him. Mak turned and held up four fingers. He pointed straight ahead and lifted two fingers then pointed around the side of the building where two of the men disappeared and indicated two more. Teriff nodded and took off around the side of the building. Mak was just moving in on his two when the ground shook and the sound of an intense explosion from inside the warehouse sounded.

"Shit!" one of the men said under his breath. "That is the third damn explosion in there. I'm not getting anything but static on my ear piece. Are you getting anything?"

"Shut the fuck up and listen. I heard gunfire too," the second man bit out. "We're not getting paid enough to go in and find out what the hell is going on. We were told not to let anyone in or out unless it was cleared. I'm sticking my ass right here where it is safer."

"Hold up, I'm getting something," the first guy muttered. "Shit, they need backup. Seems the bitch is setting off some kind of fucking explosives. She's killed four guys, but they say she is hurt."

The guy turned to look at his partner when he didn't reply. His eyes opened wide and he fumbled to bring his gun around at the beast coming at him but it was already too late. He could see his own death in the silver flames. He opened his mouth to scream, but no sound came out. His hands instinctively went to his throat, his gun clattering uselessly to the ground. He dropped to the ground dead.

"She is not a bitch, she is my mate," Mak snarled out in rage.

His eyes moved to the warehouse. He could see the glow of flames through the tinted glass. Smoke drifted out from under the door. His eyes followed along the outside wall of the warehouse until he saw a side door. Running over to it, he jerked the door off the frame, tossing it behind him. He was in such a rage at the knowledge Tansy was hurt, he was beyond thinking rationally. His only thought was to get to her.

Je talli, where are you? Mak fiercely demanded.

Mak... Tansy's faint tearful voice whispered.

Where are you, je talli? Mak asked as he moved into the smoked filled space.

His eyes narrowed on the burning remains of a large transport. He could see the remains of at least one man. He smelled the mixture of blood and burnt flesh.

He narrowed his eyes as he saw his father coming in from another entrance at the far side of the warehouse. He met his father's eyes for a moment before they both moved with the speed of their kind. Mak heard a man shouting for some of the men to get up to the upper level.

Several groups of men were climbing up the remains of a staircase while others were running to another set of stairs on the far side. He could see three up on the top level already moving slowly toward the end of the upper level where a small room opened up. Shouts burst from the men as the ones on the staircase jumped over the side. They did not make it before another explosion destroyed the staircase. Twisted metal hung suspended in the air. Three of the men were thrown a good ten feet by the explosion. Mak took care to make sure they never got up again.

~

"Tansy," Craig yelled out from behind a thick metal beam. "Give up. You aren't going to get out of here alive."

Craig wiped at the blood and sweat burning his eyes. How the fuck did she have so many explosives on her? He didn't know where the fuck she had them hidden considering the dress she was wearing. And where the hell was Drew?

He saw the asshole running for the door after the explosion. He was going to have his cowardly ass assassinated for running. He wouldn't hesitate killing either one of them. He should have done it years ago.

"Kill her!" Craig shouted out to the men on the upper level. "Blow her up if you have to but I want to see the remains to know she is really dead."

Craig watched as eight of the men moved along the narrow catwalk above him. His eyes widened when he saw a dark shadow moving up behind the group. He blinked his eyes again to clear them. What the fuck was that? He raised his good arm and aimed. He fired a shot, but the shadow had already moved beyond where he was aiming.

"Behind you!" Craig shouted out before he felt a hand wrap around his throat.

Craig was jerked roughly around. He dropped the gun in his left hand and grasped at the hand with his good hand. Choking, he looked in horror at the dark silver flames blazing in the eyes of the largest man he had ever seen in his life. The dark face and short dark hair were clearly etched in stone.

Teriff held the man responsible for harming his new daughter. He would not kill him. That privilege would go to Mak. Teriff slid a translator up to the man's ear and inserted it. He wanted this human male to know what the leader of the Prime had to say.

"You have harmed my new daughter. The Right of Justice falls to my son to kill you. You have been sentenced to death," Teriff said with a grin, letting his canines extend so Craig could see just what devil he had woken up. "I look forward to watching him kill you."

Craig stared in horror at the creature in front of him. "What the fuck are you?" he choked out hoarsely.

"Your judge," Teriff said with a grin, enjoying the stark terror scenting the man.

Teriff squeezed his hand until the man he had pinned against the metal beam went limp. He would make sure this one went back with them. He quickly secured the man to make sure he did not go anywhere.

Teriff was finished with human males. From the few he had met, they were dangerous creatures that had no appreciation for the male's right and responsibility to protect the more fragile female.

Maybe this was why these human women, who appeared so delicate and fragile, were in fact fierce and strong. All he knew was he would not tolerate any human male besides Angus Bell. He would never let any human male near his family again.

Teriff turned as he heard gunfire from up above. He saw Mak moving through the group with a cold efficiency. Bodies flew over the railing as he quickly dispatched with one after another.

Teriff looked around to see if Derik had appeared yet. He knew his younger son was after one of the men who had tried to escape. When he had gone around the side of the warehouse after the other two men Mak had seen, there had actually been three men.

Though, two of them seemed to be roughing up the other one. He had quickly dispatched with the two men, but the third had escaped. Derik was pursuing him and would take care of him.

He watched as the last body fell. He was proud of his son. He was a true warrior. Teriff knew the challenges his son had faced. He knew of the rejection of the females because of his son's size and strength. He watched the fear in the eyes of the other warriors when he walked by for the same reason.

When Tresa insisted he be allowed to travel to the human world, he had been resistant. Not because he worried about his son's safety or even Terra's. He knew he could protect them both. He worried for his son's heart. Only his family knew of the warm heart that beat under the intimidating skin of his second son.

Watching the fierce rage in his son's face as he fought to protect his mate gave Teriff an appreciation for his own mate's wisdom. She told him that Mak had found his bond mate. Teriff gave thanks to the gods and goddesses who worked in their own ways. He was proud that his second son had found a female fierce enough to match him.

CHAPTER TWENTY-ONE

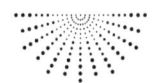

Mak's shoulders heaved as he fought to calm the fire burning through him. Bodies littered the upper and lower levels. He had shown no mercy as he cleared a path to his mate. He turned in a tight circle to make sure there were no other threats before he moved to the location the men were so focused on.

Tansy je talli, talk to me, Mak said urgently.

He felt his fear increase when she did not reply. He stopped at the door. His eyes scanned the small room, narrowing on the dark streak on the wall before he followed it down to the figure lying still on the cold, hard floor.

A curse escaped him as he rushed forward and knelt beside the inert figure. He gently rolled her over, swearing even louder when he felt the slick blood on his hand. His fingers trembled as he pushed her heavy mane of red hair away from her face so he could see if she was still breathing.

"Tansy, *je talli,*" Mak whispered as he felt the faint pulse beating in her neck. "What have you done this time, you stubborn human female?"

Tansy's eyelashes fluttered against her pale, cold cheeks. "Mak," a faint whisper sounded before her eyes opened slowly.

"I am here," Mak said gruffly, tearing the sleeve of her gown away from the wound in her arm.

"I thought you had left me," she whispered faintly.

Mak's eyes flashed with rage. "Never! And when you are well, I am going to whip your ass for this little stunt. Never again, Tansy. Never again will you go off on your own."

Tansy fought to keep her eyes open, but she was so cold and tired. It was too much for her. Her lips curved in a small smile as she felt Mak apply one of those miracle pain patches to her neck.

I really need to get a case of the damn stuff to keep on hand, she thought tiredly.

"No, you do not," Mak grunted out. "You will not need it if I keep you tied to my bed."

Tansy didn't even bother opening her eyes. She didn't think she could open them even if she wanted to. She simply turned her head into his hand and sighed.

"Okay," she replied softly before she let the darkness take her again.

∽

"When is she going to wake up?" a voice complained. "She's been asleep forever!"

"Tink, quit bouncing on the bed," Mak's deep voice said sternly. "I told you not to come here yet."

"Of course we were going to come," another feminine voice said with a hint of humor in it. "We Bell girls do what we want when we want."

"I have to agree with that," a male laughed before soft giggles and the sound of kissing teased Tansy's ears.

"Oh God, there they go again! Will you two get a room!" a soft voice said from the other side of her.

Tansy fought through the layers of cotton in her head. She turned her head toward the last voice and forced her eyes to open. Hannah sat next to her. At least, Tansy thought it was Hannah. The girl sitting next to her looked like the old Hannah she remembered.

There was a soft glow to her face and her eyes were bright with happiness.

"Personally, I think your parents have the right idea," a deeper voice replied.

Tansy's eyes widened as a male pulled Hannah up off the bed and into his arms. From the soft moan her big sister was giving, she was definitely not upset about him kissing her. Tansy's head jerked around when she heard the dark groan of another man. Where in the hell was she? Grand Central Station?

I do not know this Grand Central Station, but I am about ready to kick them all out, Mak's relieved tone echoed softly through her mind.

"I think they all need to get their own rooms," Tansy replied huskily. "Where am I?"

Tilly let out a soft cry while Tink bounced up and down on the bed in excitement. Hannah turned but remained held tightly in the arms of the man who had been kissing her passionately. Tansy noted the flushed, pink glow to Hannah's cheeks and the contented smile on her face as she leaned back into the man's arms.

"You are in our bedroom on the island I told you that was near Borj's house," Mak said in exasperation.

He couldn't get near his mate with all the females crowding around her. They had arrived unexpectedly this morning. Personally, he was ready to kick them all out. He had been waiting impatiently for his mate to finally awaken. The healers had assured him she would survive but that her body and mind were exhausted and needed additional time to heal before she would.

He had returned to his world the minute he gathered Tansy's unconscious form into his arms. His father had returned shortly after with the body of the unconscious male who had betrayed Tansy.

The man was now dead. Mak had demanded the Right of Justice. To be fair, their healers had healed the male before he fought him. The man's pleas for mercy fell on deaf ears as Mak took his time killing him. By the end, the man was begging for death. Even then, Mak did not let it come too quickly. He wanted the man to feel the same pain as what he had ordered others to do.

There was still one more male he had needed to find. The one called Drew. It had taken a few days, but RITA was very good at locating people who did not want to be found. She discovered him through the cameras that were located throughout Tansy's world. Mak had visited him at the dirty hotel he was hiding at. He had taken him to the same isolated warehouse they had used when they tried to kill his mate. Mak made sure the man suffered the same fate as his mate's first love.

"Oh, sweetheart, you gave your dad, me, and your sisters an awful scare," Tilly said tenderly as she brushed Tansy's hair back from her face. "When I first saw you…" her tearful voice faded away.

"I knew you could kick some ass, but Teriff told us how you were blowing the bad guys up and…," Tink said, shifting until she was sitting and looking down at Tansy with wide eyes. "Did you know I killed a bad guy? It was totally gross. I got this really yucky green goop all over my favorite hammer. It was some type of…." Tink gasped as she was physically lifted off the bed into a pair of huge arms.

"I think it is time we gave your sister and my brother a few moments alone," J'kar said with a dark flash of his eyes.

"But, I was telling Tansy about…" Tink began.

J'kar brushed a firm kiss across her mouth. "I know. I do not like remembering you being in danger," he replied quietly. "I need you."

Tink's face flushed and her eyes lit up. "Are you horny again?" she whispered loud enough that everyone could hear her.

J'kar looked at Tilly and Angus, and gave them an apologetic smile. "The chemicals released by her pregnancy have a very positive effect on me," he explained sheepishly.

Angus laughed and pulled Tilly into his arms. "Don't worry about it. The same thing happened to me when Tilly was pregnant. Why do you think we ended up with three girls so close together? I thought she was the most beautiful thing I'd ever seen when she was rounded with them. Still has the same effect on me now," Angus said as he buried his nose in Tilly's shoulder.

"Oh, you! You are such a romantic!" Tilly giggled.

"I can understand, as well," Borj said quietly wrapping his hands protectively around Hannah's waist so they covered the slight swell.

Tansy gasped. "You too?" she asked in wonder.

Hannah smiled down at Tansy before she leaned over and brushed a kiss across her forehead. "He makes me feel complete," Hannah whispered to Tansy. "I'm not afraid anymore."

Tansy stared deeply into her older sister's eyes, searching for the truth in her words. What she saw brought new tears to her eyes. She saw the truth in Hannah's eyes. There were no more shadows. There was no fear. There was just a warm happiness and love. She looked over Hannah's shoulder at the man standing so protectively behind her big sister. The look in his eyes promised he would always protect Hannah.

Tansy nodded, unable to say anything over the lump in her throat. She turned her head, seeking Mak. She needed to feel him. She needed him to hold her and make her feel that same sense of freedom.

I am here, je talli, Mak said tenderly.

Tansy stretched her arm out to him. She loved the feel of his large hand wrapping around hers. Neither one of them noticed the room growing quieter as everyone left. Nor did they notice as Tilly and Angus looked on with tears in their eyes as the huge, alien male gently scooped their little girl up in his massive arms and held her like she was the most precious thing in the universe. Angus pulled his wife closer and quietly closed the door to the bedroom. Pulling her down the hall to the living area where everyone else had escaped to, he paused and pulled her to him so he could feel her tiny form pressed against his.

"She'll be alright now," he murmured as quiet sobs shook Tilly's tiny figure.

"I was so afraid we would lose her," Tilly cried softly into Angus' chest. "I was afraid we would end up…"

"Shush," Angus said, breaking off her tortured words with his lips. "Someone out there was looking out for both of them. All three of our girls will be safe, loved, and protected from now on."

Tilly looked up into the eyes of the man who had captured her heart so many years ago. He might not have the build of a warrior. He might not have the physical strength of a warrior. But, he had the heart of one and that was all that mattered.

"I love you, Angus Bell," Tilly said. "I love you so much."

"I love you more, Tilly Bell," Angus said with a soft groan. "I have from the first moment you kidnapped me."

CHAPTER TWENTY-TWO

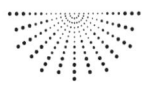

Tansy held on to Mak's huge shoulders wrapping her arms tightly around his neck and burying her face. She felt like she could stay like that forever. She had been so sure she was going to die back there in the warehouse. The thought of what happened had her reluctantly pulling away.

"What happened?" Tansy asked huskily. "Craig?"

"He is dead, as is the one called Drew," Mak said quietly, holding Tansy against him.

He shifted just enough so he could rest against the headboard of the bed. He would never admit to how tired he was. He had kept a vigil over Tansy, leaving her only to seek justice on the two males who had sought to harm her. He still needed to find the one called Avilov. The male had not been seen so far.

"What happened to them?" Tansy asked, leaning back so she could look into Mak's eyes.

"My father incapacitated the male called Craig in the warehouse. He brought him back to our world so I could demand the Right of Justice against him for harming you. My father, Derik, and I killed the others," Mak continued, deep in thought.

He did not mention something happened to his brother, Derik, back at the warehouse. Derik would not say what it was, but whatever happened had changed his cheerful, energetic little brother into a solemn, quiet warrior. He had not had much time since their return to talk to him, but he planned on doing it soon.

"You said Drew was dead too?" Tansy asked, rubbing her hand up under Mak's loose shirt.

Mak pulled Tansy even closer. "Yes. RITA was able to track him down. I killed him," Mak said in a voice that told Tansy she would get nothing else about what happened out of him. "The only one left is Avilov. RITA has been unable to get anything about him so far. He appears to have disappeared."

"What about Helene and Natasha?" she asked, concerned for her new friends.

Mak looked grim for a moment. "Rico is still looking for Natasha. They were able to rescue Helene, but the men who took Natasha have disappeared with her. Brock remained behind with Rico. He refused to return without her," Mak stated quietly.

"What else are you not telling me?" she asked determinedly.

"Merrick is missing," Mak said gruffly. "He went after some of the men who were shooting at us. Some of Rico's men retraced where he went, but they could find nothing but the dead bodies of the men who tried to kill the team members. It is as if he disappeared into thin air."

"What about his portal device?" Tansy asked, concerned. "Wouldn't he be able to use it to get back home?"

Mak shook his head. "No, Cosmos felt it was too dangerous for us to carry on our body. He had Merrick's."

Tansy felt a wave of sadness and unease at the thought of the big, alien male being lost or held captive on her home world. If any government or some crazy research agency discovered him, it would not be good. She needed to return to her world to finish one last thing. Maybe she could ask for help in return.

Tansy's hand paused from where she was stroking Mak's chest. "There is one more thing to do. I have to see the President of my country. It is imperative that he knows of the danger to him," Tansy stressed quietly.

"I thought you said your handler and the head of the CPAT knew this information," Mak bit out sharply, unwilling to let his mate return to her world.

"They don't know about this," she replied. "I couldn't take the chance of it being covered up. I have to give it to the President himself."

Mak released a deep sigh of resignation. "Very well, but be warned, it will be done my way this time," he said sternly.

Tansy looked intently at him for a moment before she nodded. "Agreed, we do this your way," she said, snuggling up against him.

Mak grinned over her head. "In that case, the first thing we do is get you naked. I have missed you."

Tansy couldn't help the chuckle that escaped. "What about the living room full of family we have?"

Mak grunted and pulled away, untangling her arms from around his waist and inside his shirt. "Wait here," he responded in a determined tone.

Tansy giggled as she watched him heading with a determined stride for the door. It opened and he disappeared down the hallway. Shaking her head, she slipped from the bed. She knew he wanted her to remain in it, but she needed to go to the bathroom and she desperately wanted a shower.

She stood up and was surprised to find her legs were only a little bit shaky. She pushed her heavy mane of hair back from her face and headed for the door that looked like it led to the bathroom. She grinned in delight when she saw the huge, bright, airy room.

It was as big as her bedroom back home. On one side was a double vanity and what looked like a toilet. Along one wall was a huge tub, but it was the shower that held her mesmerized. It looked like it was made out of smooth coral. There were no sides, no curtains, nothing.

The wall behind it showed a vast ocean of purple and blue. Soft pink sand covered the beach and tall trees swayed as a gentle breeze caressed them. Tansy couldn't think of anything but standing in the beautiful shower and gazing at what could only be paradise in her mind. She had found her deserted, well, almost deserted, island.

She laughed as she heard Mak's muffled roar for everyone to leave. He wanted to be alone with his mate and he wanted everyone gone....

now. Since she didn't hear anyone yelling back at him, she had to assume he got what he wanted.

Tansy let the lightweight pale green gown she was wearing fall to the floor in a pile around her feet. She stepped out of it and into the shower unit. The moment she did, a light rain of warm water fell from the ceiling. She raised her face, closing her eyes as she did, and let the warm water wash away all the fear, heartache, and sorrow. It was time for a new beginning. For the first time, she felt like she could begin fresh. She could have the life she always dreamed about but never dared to believe she would have.

She started when she felt a pair of rough, calloused hands grip her hips and pull her back against a hard, long length. A moan escaped as she felt Mak's hard cock jerk in response to her. She would have turned around, but he tightened his hands, forcing her to remain still.

"Does your dream include younglings?" Mak murmured quietly.

Tansy tilted her head back and stared up into his dark silver eyes. "What if it does?" she responded seriously. "What if it includes children and long days and nights together and growing old?"

"Then, I think we need to get started," Mak whispered, looking down into her dark green eyes. "We have a lot to do and I plan on enjoying every minute of it… forever and ever."

This time when Tansy tried to turn around, he let her. Picking her up, he waited as her long legs wrapped around his waist before he slowly lowered her until she was impaled on his thick shaft. Both of them moaned as they came together. Mak began rocking gently at first, lifting her up before letting her slide back down onto him.

"Gods Tansy, I love you," he said hoarsely as he began rocking faster and faster. "I need you."

"I love you, too," she moaned in return. "Forever, Mak. You promised me forever and I want every damn second of it."

Mak let his canines lower. He would do everything in his power to gift her with a child. He wanted to see her body swell like her sisters. He wanted to feel their child growing inside her. He wanted her. Just the thought of her swollen with his seed was enough to push him over the top. He shuddered as he felt the strong release. Tilting Tansy's head to the side, he bit down on the curve between her neck and shoulder, releasing the chemical into his mate. Her body reacted almost violently to his, clamping down as if determined to suck every bit of his seed from his body.

"Yes," he roared out passionately.

Tansy gasped as she felt the hot waves of his release spill inside of her, triggering her own violent reaction. She could feel her vaginal walls pulsing around him. She buried her face into his shoulder and bit down to keep the scream from erupting. A sob rose up as intense emotions threatened to overwhelm her.

"Don't ever leave me," she begged. "I thought you had left me back at the warehouse when I couldn't reach you. I never want to feel that emptiness again. Please, don't ever leave me," she whispered as he reluctantly pulled his mouth away from her delicate skin and ran a healing stroke of his tongue over the marks he left.

Mak kept his arms wrapped tightly around Tansy and stepped out of the shower. A warm burst of air rose up, drying the water on their skin. He knew she would want to dry her hair so he stood under the warm breeze a little longer while most of the moisture was removed from it. Once that was done, he walked back into their bedroom.

"You thought I had left you there?" Mak snarled out. "You thought I would leave you to those other males?"

Tansy shivered at the look in his eyes. "Well, only for a minute or two," she said, looking unsure up at him. "I mean, I couldn't connect with you and things were going to hell in a hand-basket really fast...," she tried to explain. "Hell, I had been shot and was bleeding all over the place, for crying out loud. Surely you can't blame me for not thinking clearly," she added defensively.

"No, you quote 'kind-of forgot to tell me something on purpose'," Mak retaliated. "I remember telling you I was going to whip your ass for that when you were healed," he said as a determined gleam appeared in his eyes.

Tansy's eyes widened before narrowing. "You wouldn't dare!" she hissed back.

"Wouldn't I?" Mak said as he pulled a strap from under the mattress. "Prime males use these to restrain their females until the mating chemical in our bite takes effect and they are ready to mate with us. Since that is not a requirement with you, I will be using them to remind you what happens when you do not listen to me," he said with a smile as he fastened the straps around both of her wrists.

"You can't do this," she muttered as she tried to buck him off of her. That was kind of hard to do since they were still connected from the shower. "Mak! I mean it! You can't discipline me! I was doing my job. I was doing what I was trained to do," she added with a moan as he pulled out of her.

Mak ignored her demands to be released. Instead, he reached for the leg straps. He hooked them to the end of the bed. Reaching for one delicate ankle, he quickly bound first one then the other.

Once she was spread open for him, he reached into the drawer next to their bed and removed a small device. He smiled as he flicked the button and a small laser light appeared. He gently ran it over her mound, leaving only a small, narrow strip of soft, downy hair.

He had dreamed of doing this from the first moment he saw her naked. He loved the gasps and moans that filled the air of their bedroom as he worked her body. He would build her up until she would promise to never put her life in danger again. Only when he had exacted that promise would he give her fulfillment.

"What are you doing?" she asked dazed.

"I am disciplining you," he replied as he set the hair removal device back in the drawer.

"I thought you said you were going to whip my ass," she asked breathlessly, looking up into his flaming silver eyes.

"Oh, I'm going to," he replied as he ran one finger along her swollen lips. "I am going to whip your ass until you beg me to take it. I'm going to make you scream over and over until you will do anything I ask of you."

"I was trained to withstand torture," she replied in a husky voice filled with need. "I'll never scream or give in."

Mak's smile was patient as he gazed down at her. "I wouldn't bet on that," he responded lightly as he held up a lightweight silver chain with several rounded clips that looked almost like silver hoop earrings. "I think we will start with these."

Tansy's shocked gasp turned to a smothered cry of pleasure/pain as Mak clamped down on her right nipple, sucking it into a tight, swollen nub. Once it was puckered into a tight pebble, he slid the fine end through her nipple leaving the small ring attached. He did the same thing to her left nipple, enjoying the way her body bowed into his as he pierced each nipple.

"Oh god," she moaned as he attached the chain to them and pulled.

She tried to pull her legs together to relieve the sudden burning she was feeling between them. It was as if her body was catching on fire, demanding she see how much it could handle before she exploded. She bit her lip in a determined attempt to keep the plea from escaping.

"Not yet, *je talli*," Mak murmured, pulling the chain back and forth gently. "You were a very, very bad mate for not listening to me. You caused me to suffer much fear from your behavior. I want you to know and remember what happens when you do not listen to me."

Tansy shook her head back and forth, biting her lip instead of replying to his reasoning. Her body rose up again off the covers as he flicked the swollen nub she couldn't hide from him. Her deep gasp of breath told him how much she liked it; just as the hot moisture that pooled between her legs, causing the soft, swollen folds to grow slick with need.

"Mak," she began, but he silenced her with his lips.

He did not want her to beg too soon. He wanted to take his time and enjoy every inch of her delicious curves. If she began to beg for him to take her now, he would. He was barely holding on to the little bit of self-control he had. She had no idea how beautiful she looked tied to his bed, swollen and scenting of arousal. Her scent alone was enough to drive him over the edge. Right now, he was taking quick deep breaths through his mouth, but that wasn't working. He could almost taste her need in the air.

He had to finish what he started. He had to make her understand that when she didn't listen to him or at least work with him, she endangered both their lives. He had to show her what their life could be like together so she never wanted to take a chance of their being apart.

With a growl, he pushed back away from her lips and moved down her body in a concentrated attack on her senses. He licked, kissed, and stroked every inch of her. He moved down her legs, took his time releasing more of the mating chemical as he marked the inside of her thigh, before he let his mouth hover over the slick lips of her pussy.

"I am going to taste you," he whispered. "I'm going to drink you down. Then, I am going to turn you over and fuck you hard."

Tansy was gasping as she listened to what he was planning to do to her. Her whole body was one throbbing nerve. Every touch pulled at her, taking her to such a height that she felt like she was about to shatter at any moment. She didn't see how anything else he did could take her any further up the pinnacle of heaven than what he had done so far.

"Please," the soft whimper burst from her raw throat. "Please…"

Mak ignored the soft word, burying his face between her slick folds and nipping them when they tightened in response. Tansy's hoarse cry drove him on. He pulled the swollen folds back, attacking her protected core with his rough tongue. He drank, licked, and feasted until she screamed out, convulsing around him as she shattered.

He waited as she came down from her climax. He stroked her throbbing vaginal walls with his thick fingers, drawing her climax out before he pulled them out. Now, he would let her know what it felt like to be truly taken. With her body throbbing from desire, he would build her up again and again until she melted into him as one.

Mak sat up and gripped Tansy's small waist in his hands. He would need to be careful. He would need to balance the pain with the pleasure. He turned her over before she realized what he was doing and pulled her up onto her hands and knees as far as the restraints would allow. Holding her around the waist, he let his hand fall on her smooth, lush ass with a slight sting.

"What the…" Tansy cried out at the stinging blow to her ass. "Mak, what are you doing?"

He brought his hand down on the other rounded cheek, watching as it turned red with his handprint. Tansy cried out again, fighting the restraints now. He leaned forward and pulled gently on the chain swinging from her nipples.

"Oh!" she cried out, arching into the tug.

"I told you I was going to whip your ass," he said huskily, bringing his hand down again a little harder, then rubbing the spot to take out the sting. "Let me. You will see it can be enjoyable."

"If you think it is so enjoyable, let me spank your ass!" Tansy bit out, even as she tilted her ass up to take another slap. She moaned out as he brought his hand down again and again.

Mak knew she was ready when she lowered her head down to the mattress and waited for another stinging slap. Instead, he positioned himself behind her and forced his cock between her slick folds, not stopping until he was buried balls deep inside her. He reached over and wound her thick red hair around the palm of his right hand while he used his left hand to rub her.

He moved deep, hard, and fast, giving her no mercy as he took his own pleasure while giving her the same. He pulled on her hair, forcing her to rise up. The angle forced his cock deeper. A deep shaking began inside him as his climax built to an explosion that tore a cry from deep inside him.

"Forever!" he yelled out hoarsely. "You are mine forever!"

Tansy's own pleading gasps echoed his as she came again. She was beyond thinking. She had shattered long ago. She had also realized what he meant that one could not survive without the other.

The concept had been so foreign to her before. Now, she understood what Mak had been trying to tell her all along. They were bound together with a bond so strong and yet so fragile that if one were to perish so would the other. They were no longer two separate entities, but two halves of one whole.

"Forever," Tansy promised as exhaustion took her and she descended into a deep, dreamless sleep.

Mak slowly released his mate, lowering her body gently to the bed. He refused to feel remorse at taking her so soon after her waking. He knew he needed to seal his claim on her before she had a chance to reconsider or think it possible for her to break the bond connecting them. He let his hand move to rest for a moment over her stomach. If the Gods and Goddesses were looking on, he was sure they would have blessed him and his mate with a child.

Or two if her sisters were any indication of how Prime males and human females bred, Mak thought with a contented grin as he pulled the covers over them.

He pulled his mate's sedated body into his, enjoying the feel of her lush curves. He closed his eyes and gave a sigh. He let his mind connect with his mate so he could monitor her in case she needed him. The moment he touched her, a wave of warmth flooded him. A curve tilted the corner of his mouth even as sleep overtook his tired body.

CHAPTER TWENTY-THREE

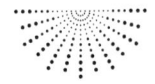

The President of the United States sat back at his desk in the Oval Office looking over the new documents that had been placed for his review. He ran a weary hand through his hair and loosened the tie around his neck.

With a muttered curse, he pulled the tie free and tossed it over the back of his chair with his jacket. Standing, he stretched before moving over to the windows overlooking the front lawn. The vice-president was pushing for him to agree with attacking a country in the Middle East that was still considered one of their allies. Lately, he had been getting a feeling of unease with some of the reports he had been receiving from his second-in-command. He turned around, determined to review the report again.

He was just sitting down when he jerked back in alarm as a shimmering doorway appeared in the middle of his office. He moved to reach for the alarm mounted under his desk, but some instinct told him to wait. His hand hovered over the button as he waited to see who or what came through the opening.

His eyes widened as three very petite but very beautiful women walked through. A split second later, they were followed by a small group of huge males. Askew Thomas' eyes widened as he took in the size of the males towering over the females. The female with the long red hair turned and scowled at the men.

"Quit trying to be so... so bossy!" she was saying as she glared at the largest man.

"Oh, you can forget it!" the smallest female said, rolling her eyes. "J'kar is about to have a heart attack just because I insisted on coming with you. Like he thought I would miss an opportunity to meet the President!"

One of the men said something in a low tone which drew a snort of laughter out of all the women. The oldest woman turned and smiled at Askew as he sat frozen with his hand wavering above the button. She took a hesitant step forward.

"Mr. President, my name is Tilly Bell. These are two of my daughters, Jasmine and Tansy. Tansy works," Tilly was saying before a low growl behind her stopped her. She rolled her eyes before continuing. "Tansy *used* to work for the government in a special program."

"Mom, I can speak for myself," Tansy said, ignoring Mak's attempt to pull her back behind him. "Knock it off!" she muttered under her breath. "He's the friggin' president, not an operative."

Tilly smiled apologetically to Askew, who was still sitting looking at the strange group standing in front of him. Rising up out of his seat, he decided to trust his instincts that they meant no harm to him. It was obvious the three females were human. It was equally obvious that the four males were not.

"Perhaps you should begin again," Askew said, moving around his desk so he could stand in front of Tilly.

Tansy took a step forward, ignoring Mak's silent threat to whip her ass again. "It might help if you allow us to insert a translator so you can understand everything that is being said," Tansy began quietly. "It doesn't hurt, nor will it do anything other than translate between our language and theirs."

Tansy stood still waiting for the president to decide whether he would allow them to insert the translator or not. She kept his gaze, determined to show she would not waver. The President's eyes moved from her to the four men with intense silver eyes.

He studied each carefully. His gaze paused on the oldest male who looked back at him arrogantly. It was obvious all four men were used to commanding others, but the oldest male held that to an even higher level. It was obvious he was used to being in charge.

Askew looked at Tansy and gave a brief nod. He knew who she was. Her name was on the report he had been given. It had identified her as being a traitor and extremely dangerous. She was implicated in everything from drug running, to delivering weapons to their enemies, to human trafficking. Looking into her clear green eyes and determined face, he didn't believe a single thing in the report.

Borj stepped closer to the President and held up a small device. He indicated he was going to place it near his ear. Askew remained still, waiting as the huge man placed the device against his ear. Within seconds, the man took a step away from him and bowed his head.

"Mr. President, my name is Borj 'Tag Krell Manok. I am an ambassador for our world," Borj straightened and nodded to the men behind him. "May I present my oldest brother, J'kar. He commands our warships along with my brother Mak," Borj said, waving a hand to the largest man Askew had ever seen. Borj turned and nodded to the oldest man. "May I also present Teriff 'Tag Krell Manok, my father and the leader of all Prime Clans and our world of Baade."

Askew swallowed as he realized he was in the middle of something nothing in his experience had prepared him for. He was being introduced to aliens. He fought a wave of terror. His eyes swung around to the three small women standing near the men. They appeared to see nothing wrong with the entire situation.

"Oh, you poor dear," Tilly said, moving up to Askew. "They really aren't as big and bad as they look," she said, looking behind her at the men. "Well, they are, but only if you piss them off," she said cheerfully.

"Mom, you are not helping the situation," Tansy muttered.

"I thought she did a good job," Tink protested. "I mean, it's not like they are the Juggernauts or anything."

"That is Juangan," J'kar corrected, coming to stand closer to Tink.

"Whatever!" she said cheerfully. "The Juangans are these really huge lizard looking creatures that eat everyone, including each other. The cool thing is if you pop them on the head with a hammer their skulls crack like a walnut."

"Tink, you are not helping the situation either," Tansy said in exasperation. "I really should have come alone."

"No!" Four very angry male voices echoed loudly through the room.

One of the doors to the Oval Office opened and two of the president's security force rushed in. They stumbled to a stop when Mak snarled at them. They drew their weapons, staring at the four huge males who were standing protectively around the women.

"Leave us!" Askew ordered. "Now! And not a word to anyone on this until I debrief you."

"Sir..." one of the men began.

"That's an order," Askew said, moving so that he was standing between his men and his visitors. "Wait for me outside, and do not let anyone, and I mean anyone, enter."

"Yes, sir," the man replied, looking with uncertainty at the small group.

Once the door was closed, Askew walked over to the small bar set up along the wall. He poured himself a drink before he raised it with a questioning look. Teriff smiled and took a step forward.

"We would enjoy sharing refreshments with you," Teriff said with a smile. "What are you called, human?"

"Askew Thomas," Askew replied, handing a drink to Teriff.

"I have been called a 'grandfather' and a 'dickhead' by my new youngest daughter, but you may call me Teriff," Teriff replied, downing the drink in one swig.

Askew bit back a bark of laughter as he watched the youngest girl's face turn a bright red. "I only called you that because you were being mean to me and I just found out I was pregnant with twins! You can't hold it against me forever," Tink said, moving to sit down on one of the couches.

Before she could sit, one of the huge males, the one called J'kar, reached for her and pulled her down on his lap. He appeared to be trying to calm her from the urgent whispers being muttered. Whatever he said must have worked because she turned her face into his shoulder and nodded quietly.

"Mr. President, I have some very important information I need to share with you," Tansy said quietly, walking over to hand the President a flash drive. "I worked as an operative with CPAT until recently. I uncovered information that is vital to the country and to your personal safety. There was no one I could fully trust with delivering the information I have. It has all been checked out. I want you to know I would do whatever it takes to ensure your safety and that of my country," Tansy finished.

Askew took the flash drive from Tansy, turning it over in his hand several times before he said anything. "I would like to see this now, if you don't mind," he said quietly.

"Not at all," came the equally quiet response.

Forty minutes later, Askew was standing in the exact position he had been in before his surprise visitors appeared. Only this time he was more appreciative of the unease that had been driving him. It would appear it was well founded. He had no doubt at all the information he just reviewed was genuine. Just as there was not a doubt in his mind that the men in this room were indeed aliens from another world.

Borj had quietly answered his questions about Baade. He had explained there were other species in the universe. He assured Askew they had no desire to invade their world, nor did any other species.

At the moment, Earth was considered an undesirable world to visit and much too distant to make it feasible for most of the species. Borj refused to explain how the gateway worked or about the technology behind it, stating it was better for the Earth if that knowledge wasn't available at this time.

"We are much more advanced than your world in many ways," Teriff added. "It is best if things remain as they are. We have no desire to change your world. We only look for women who are bond mates to our males."

"You aren't keeping them for just breeding, are you?" Askew asked, concerned as his eyes moved to the rounded swell on Tink.

J'kar growled in a low, menacing tone at Askew. "Do not insult my mate."

"Down boy, I think he just wants to make sure you guys aren't using us as an incubator," Tink giggled before turning to Askew. "No, this is pure and simple love. I love the big guy and he loves me. I'm very happy."

"All of my daughters are," Tilly said with a smile.

Askew looked carefully at Tilly before he asked her the question that had been on his mind since he first saw her. "You wouldn't happen to know of an Angus Bell, would you?"

Tilly's light laughter floated through the room. "I not only know him, I've been married to him for almost thirty wonderful years."

Askew leaned forward with a huge smile on his face. "I love his books! The movies are good, but his books are incredible. He is not the only one who is well known. Your work on generators and power grids are unbelievable."

Tilly blushed as the president complimented her. "Thank you."

Tansy stood up suddenly. "Mr. President, about the information I gave you…" she started to say.

Askew stood up and looked intently at Tansy. "I will take care of it immediately," he said quietly. "I would like to thank you for all that you have done for your country and for me personally. I hope that this will not be the last time I see you," he added, walking over and picking up Tansy's delicate hand in his own.

Tansy bit her lip. "There are two Prime males here. One is trying to rescue the girl I told you about. The other… the other is missing. If you hear of anything unusual… of a strange male, can you call this number and leave a message? He is a friend and we need to find him," Tansy explained as she handed the phone number for RITA over to the President.

"I'll do my best to see if I hear anything and will take immediate action if I do," Askew said, taking the number and sliding it in the front pocket of his pants.

"We need to go before anyone else tries to contact you," Mak said, beginning to feel uneasy. "If you find the man called Avilov, I claim the Right of Justice against him for his crimes."

"Right of Justice?" Askew asked, taking a step away from Mak.

"He has caused my mate great harm. It is my right to challenge him," Mak said shortly. "You will hold him until I return."

Askew nodded his head in agreement. The last thing he wanted to do was make this huge ass alien warrior mad at him. If he wanted to claim some 'Right of Justice' against Avilov, more power to him. He knew the Russian billionaire would be a hard case to prosecute. If the male wanted to take care of justice, Askew would not have a problem looking the other way.

A knock on the door echoed around the room. Teriff looked at Askew and nodded to him. "We must go. Go in peace, human," Teriff said as he pressed the portal device.

Askew watched in awe as similar shimmering doorways appeared. Within moments, he stood alone once again in his office. The sound of the continued knocking finally broke through his thoughts. Calling out for whoever was at the door to enter, he watched as the two members of his security team entered, looking around with a look of suspicion and wonder on their faces.

"I have a job for you two," Askew said sternly, looking at the picture on his computer. "This must be done with the utmost secrecy," he added, looking at his two most trusted men.

EPILOGUE

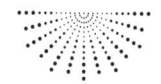

Tansy stretched out on the powder soft pink sand and sighed in contentment. She had no intentions of moving. Not even for her sisters.

She and Mak practically lived on the small island not far from where Hannah lived. It was a ten minute flight in one of the gliders to visit. Tink was still living at the palace. Her parents had taken over Mak's mountain home where her dad continued to write and her mom tinkered on her inventions. Since the birth of Tink's and Hannah's twins, they were staying at the palace as well.

It was over six months since they had talked to the President and three weeks since they had returned to Earth to check on things. Merrick had been found since their last visit. Right now, he was trying to keep the small female he brought back with him from escaping.

Tansy decided she had enough on her plate. She didn't want to get involved. She would let them work it out. She was too busy being a beach bum, a very pregnant one at that. She glanced over at Hannah, who was sitting under the shade of one of the trees. She had Tansy's newest niece at her breast while her nephew lay cooing up at the leaves moving above him.

Tink was playing in the surf with some of the sea dragons that liked to come up close to shore. She squealed loudly as one of them squirted her with water. She came up out of the water splashing back at them as she moved up onto the warm sand to plop down next to Tansy.

She shook the water from her short curls, ignoring Tansy's startled yell. "Come on, Tansy. You should try it! It is so much fun. Just ask Hannah," Tink said, bringing up an ongoing argument.

Tansy opened her eyes and glared at Tink. "No!" she said shortly before she closed her eyes again.

"Come on! Pretty please, just once," Tink pleaded. "Hannah and I'll do it too, so you won't be alone, won't we Hannah?"

Hannah moved little Ocean to her shoulder so she could burp her. "I'm game, but you know Tresa is going to have her hands full if I do," she said, smiling as Ocean let out a huge belch of gas.

"Teriff can help her and you know mom and dad are here too," Tink said excitedly. "See, even Hannah is game."

Tansy sat up with a sigh of resignation. *So much for being on a deserted island,* she thought. It did absolutely no good if your family knew where you were and insisted on constantly visiting you. Maybe if she did this, J'kar would drag Tink back to the palace.

"Okay," Tansy said. "Are you sure they won't mind watching two sets of twins? Tink, your two are a handful now that they are crawling and getting into everything."

"Teriff acts like he is the only one who can control them," Tink laughed, waving her hand in the air. "All he has to do is lay down on the floor and they are all over him. He loves being such a 'grandfather' to those two."

"He is already threatening all the warriors he is going to be the one to kill any of them who have sons who look at his granddaughters," Hannah said, laying Ocean next to her brother, Sky.

"Okay, I give in. What do I do?" Tansy asked, flipping her long braid over her shoulder.

"All you have to do is picture what you would like to do to Mak in your head," Tink said excitedly. "I picture all the wicked things I can imagine and the next thing you know, J'kar is panting and growling and..." her voice faded away as Tansy raised her hand to stop her.

"Tink, that is WAY more information than I need to know about what you have going on in your head, much less what you are doing with J'kar," Tansy said drily. "Are you telling me you are having…"

"Mind sex," Hannah giggled with a blush. "It really is incredible and it does seem to have a really interesting effect on the guys."

Tansy looked back and forth between her sisters and shook her head. This is what they have been pestering her about for the past week? They want her to have mind sex with Mak? A small smile curved her lips. It wasn't like she could get pregnant. And, he did seem to find her more arousing since she was. Maybe it would be fun to see what would happen if she did.

"They're in the house with the parents, right?" Tansy asked as a mischievous smile curved her lips.

"She's in," Tink said excitedly to Hannah.

"She's in," Hannah responded with a shy grin.

"She's definitely in," Tansy said as her eyes lit up with excitement.

Five minutes later, three men and two sets of parents were hurrying out of the house. All three girls burst into laughter at the determined, strained expressions on their mate's faces. If the bulges in the front of their pants were any indication of the success of their thoughts, it might be a long, long time before Tink and Hannah's little ones saw their parents.

Tansy looked at the passion glazed eyes of her mate. He didn't say a word, just bent down and scooped her up. She squealed as he folded one of his palms over her breast and tugged on the small silver hoop still attached. Her nipple responded immediately to his possessive tug.

Oh yes, Tansy thought as Mak strode through their home, slamming the door to their bedroom behind them. *I am going to have to remember this mind sex. If I had known it would work this good, I would have done it months ago.*

Mak's soft growl flowed through her as he laid her gently down on the bed and began pulling his clothes off. Tansy stared at the man who had swept into her life, laying claim to her heart, body and soul.

He was her personal Titan; destroying any who would harm her, and protecting her, even from herself. He had laid claim to her, conquering her with his love and tearing down all her defenses.

Forever, je talli, forever, Mak's soft voice caressed her mind before she forgot everything else.

To be continued…. **Cosmos' Promise**

Cosmos Raines is one of the most brilliant inventors in the world, but his most profound discovery must be hidden from Earth's people. Already he has lost control of the intergalactic Gateway he created—his warehouse is full of alien guests! Most importantly though, he found the woman of his dreams on the other side of the Gateway, and now that they've found each other, no one is going to take her away from him—not the clan who wants to use her nor her father who thinks all human males are worthless. It may take every invention he's ever made and every bit of ingenuity he has, but this is one battle he is going to win.

Check out the full book here: books2read.com/Cosmos-Promise

Or read on for a sneak peek into a new series!

Touch of Frost
Magic, New Mexico Book 1
Sci-fi and Paranormal Fantasy collide!

When a maximum-security fugitive escapes to a distant, forbidden planet whose inhabitants have not mastered space travel yet, it's Star Ranger Frost who is sent after him.

Lacey Adams is a widow who owns an animal shelter in Magic, New Mexico… an *unusual*, small town, to say the least, and she is certainly not easily taken hostage, not by the fugitive and not by the Star Ranger who wants her for himself.

Check out the full book here: books2read.com/Touch-of-Frost

ADDITIONAL BOOKS

If you loved this story by me (S.E. Smith) please leave a review! You can discover additional books at: http://sesmithfl.com and http://sesmithya.com or find your favorite way to keep in touch here: https://sesmithfl.com/contact-me/ Be sure to sign up for my newsletter to hear about new releases!

Recommended Reading Order Lists:
http://sesmithfl.com/reading-list-by-events/
http://sesmithfl.com/reading-list-by-series/

The Series

Science Fiction / Romance

Dragon Lords of Valdier Series
It all started with a king who crashed on Earth, desperately hurt. He inadvertently discovered a species that would save his own.

Curizan Warrior Series
The Curizans have a secret, kept even from their closest allies, but even they

are not immune to the draw of a little known species from an isolated planet called Earth.

Marastin Dow Warriors Series
The Marastin Dow are reviled and feared for their ruthlessness, but not all want to live a life of murder. Some wait for just the right time to escape....

Sarafin Warriors Series
A hilariously ridiculous human family who happen to be quite formidable... and a secret hidden on Earth. The origin of the Sarafin species is more than it seems. Those cat-shifting aliens won't know what hit them!

Dragonlings of Valdier Novellas
The Valdier, Sarafin, and Curizan Lords had children who just cannot stop getting into trouble! There is nothing as cute or funny as magical, shapeshifting kids, and nothing as heartwarming as family.

Cosmos' Gateway Series
Cosmos created a portal between his lab and the warriors of Prime. Discover new worlds, new species, and outrageous adventures as secrets are unravelled and bridges are crossed.

The Alliance Series
When Earth received its first visitors from space, the planet was thrown into a panicked chaos. The Trivators came to bring Earth into the Alliance of Star Systems, but now they must take control to prevent the humans from destroying themselves. No one was prepared for how the humans will affect the Trivators, though, starting with a family of three sisters....

Lords of Kassis Series
It began with a random abduction and a stowaway, and yet, somehow, the Kassisans knew the humans were coming long before now. The fate of more than one world hangs in the balance, and time is not always linear....

Zion Warriors Series

Time travel, epic heroics, and love beyond measure. Sci-fi adventures with heart and soul, laughter, and awe-inspiring discovery...

Paranormal / Fantasy / Romance

Magic, New Mexico Series
Within New Mexico is a small town named Magic, an... unusual town, to say the least. With no beginning and no end, spanning genres, authors, and universes, hilarity and drama combine to keep you on the edge of your seat!

Spirit Pass Series
There is a physical connection between two times. Follow the stories of those who travel back and forth. These westerns are as wild as they come!

Second Chance Series
Stand-alone worlds featuring a woman who remembers her own death. Fiery and mysterious, these books will steal your heart.

More Than Human Series
Long ago there was a war on Earth between shifters and humans. Humans lost, and today they know they will become extinct if something is not done....

The Fairy Tale Series
A twist on your favorite fairy tales!

A Seven Kingdoms Tale
Long ago, a strange entity came to the Seven Kingdoms to conquer and feed on their life force. It found a host, and she battled it within her body for centuries while destruction and devastation surrounded her. Our story begins when the end is near, and a portal is opened....

Epic Science Fiction / Action Adventure

Project Gliese 581G Series
An international team leave Earth to investigate a mysterious object in our solar system that was clearly made by someone, someone who isn't from

Earth. Discover new worlds and conflicts in a sci-fi adventure sure to become your favorite!

New Adult / Young Adult

Breaking Free Series
A journey that will challenge everything she has ever believed about herself as danger reveals itself in sudden, heart-stopping moments.

The Dust Series
Fragments of a comet hit Earth, and Dust wakes to discover the world as he knew it is gone. It isn't the only thing that has changed, though, so has Dust...

ABOUT THE AUTHOR

S.E. Smith is an *internationally acclaimed, New York Times* and *USA TODAY Bestselling* author of science fiction, romance, fantasy, paranormal, and contemporary works for adults, young adults, and children. She enjoys writing a wide variety of genres that pull her readers into worlds that take them away.

Printed in Great Britain
by Amazon